Lonely is the Hunter

Outlaw Caleb Ollinger has no idea how much outrage he will stir after stopping off in the New Mexico town of Carrizozo. A few drinks and a game of poker suddenly turn into a double killing – the gambler who has been caught cheating matters little – but an innocent boy plowed down by Ollinger was the son of New Mexico's territorial governor.

Bounty hunter Chance Newcombe is hired to bring the killer in, but the loner has an ulterior motive. Chance attempts to lure Caleb's brother, Pake, into the picture, under the pretense that they will be rescuing the wayward kid. Chance comes across an old comrade at a relay station who is also after Caleb, so as to secure an amnesty granted by the governor which wipes out his past crimes. Bullets are bound to fly when the disparate protagonists finally meet up at the Hanging Tree.

Lonely is the Hunter

Dale Graham

A Black Horse Western
ROBERT HALE

© Dale Graham 2016
First published in Great Britain 2016

ISBN 978-0-7198-1986-5

The Crowood Press
The Stable Block
Crowood Lane
Ramsbury
Marlborough
Wiltshire SN8 2HR

www.crowood.com

Robert Hale is an imprint
of The Crowood Press

Printed and bound in Great Britain by
CPI Group (UK) Ltd, Croydon CR0 4YY

ONE

FROM BAD ...

Hats pulled low to shade out the searing heat, the three men plodded across the bleak undulating terrain known as the White Sands. Only the hardiest were able to survive in this vast empty wilderness of southern New Mexico. Proof of this was evident all around where the bleached bones of animals unable to find sustenance littered the harsh landscape.

Not even the resilient cactus could survive. Occasional clumps of mesquite and the ubiquitous yucca were a welcome relief from the rolling banks of endless sand dominating the monotonous landscape.

Any association with easy riding had long since faded into oblivion. For here the relentless intensity of the fire-breathing sun dragon was incessant. This was a journey no man undertook lightly. An unremitting slog. Plod, plod, plodding ever onward while sucking in hot air that scoured their raw throats. Had the travellers recognized the brutal reality on which they were engaged, common sense would surely have prevailed and they would have taken a different route.

But these men had embarked upon their journey while suffering from the effects of an over-indulgence of tequila. Turning back was not an option. It was too late for that anyway. Only now was the bleak significance of their enforced departure beginning to dawn.

'How much farther?' grunted one of the outlaws, barely above a croak.

There was no reply. Perhaps because none of them had the answer. The query was not repeated as the men trudged onward.

As the name implied, from a distance this unique landscape gave off the appearance of sand. In actuality it was pure gypsum, and even more exacting to traverse than a regular desert. Pure white reflected the full power of the sun. A blinding torment that required the travellers to hide their faces, making navigation a matter of pure luck. It was also exceedingly tough on the horses, which kept sinking into the soft powder. As a result the men had to walk them at regular intervals.

They had left the small settlement of Elephant Butte three days before under a disparaging cloud. Yet the sky overhead had remained a deep azure. The owner of the cantina had objected to their leader taking advantage of his daughter. The girl's screams behind the cantina had attracted the attention and anger of the dominant Mexican community.

Only by the skin of their teeth had Caleb Ollinger and his two buddies escaped unscathed. Without thought they had loosed off a hail of bullets to deter the irate citizens from pursuit as they rode off into the desert. Luckily none had bitten into soft flesh. Unless, that is, you counted a stray dog that had found itself on the wrong side of the dusty single street.

Indeed no pursuit would have been forthcoming as the canny Mexicans were well aware of the danger posed by the Sands. They were satisfied that nature would exact a fitting penalty on their behalf.

And after three days it appeared that the good *ciudadanos* of Elephant Butte would have their wish. Heads were drooping in communion with those of their lethargic mounts. The last of the water had been used up that morning. Desperation was scrawled across ashen features. Only a weariness induced by their desperate predicament prevented vehement condemnation of Ollinger's rash action. Yet still the oldest of the trio, Shifty Simms, felt it necessary to voice their disgruntlement.

'Why in tarnation couldn't you keep your hands to yourself, Caleb?' he grumbled through swollen lips and a dried out mouth. 'Now you've gotten us into a right mess.'

'Pake ain't gonna like it,' muttered the third man shaking his bony head. 'He's expecting us in Roswell next week.' Delta Jack had not yet come round to the notion that without water their chances of meeting up with the gang boss, and elder brother to Caleb, were decidedly slim. Their hurried departure from Elephant Butte had meant they were only carrying basic provisions. And those were now all but used up.

'D'yuh think I don't know that, lunkhead?' Caleb snapped back, trying to make excuses for his indiscretions. 'How was I to know those turkeys would kick up such a fuss over some greaser gal?'

Muttered imprecations followed. But Caleb's sidekicks figured it wise to remain silent. The kid's edgy gun hand was liable to grab hardware if pushed to the limit of his irascible temper. The outlaws were too exhausted anyway to quibble. The damage had been done, and now they would all pay the price. Gritting their teeth, all they could do was trudge onward following a northeasterly course and pray for a guardian angel to put an end to their plight.

Three months before, the Ollinger gang had split up until the heat died down following their last highly successful raid. No problems had been encountered at the Flagstaff bank, which had been robbed of a month's takings. Unless you counted a dead bank teller shot down by the younger Ollinger.

Unbeknown to the outlaws, their haul included an army payroll that made for a substantial bonus. After dividing up the take, Pake Ollinger and a half-breed Cheyenne sporting the odd handle of Ten Sleep had gone north into Colorado. Nobody knew his real name. It was Pake who gave him the label due to the breed's penchant for nodding off in the saddle. Ten hours communing with the Great Spirit was not uncommon.

Caleb and his two pals had headed for Mexico where the senoritas were more willing and the booze a sight cheaper. Tequila was Caleb's favourite tipple.

But money in the hands of outlaws is soon frittered away. Saving for a rainy day played no part in their scheme of how life should be played out. In the owl-hooter land of their dreams, the sun always shone.

In consequence, Caleb had received a letter from his brother while sojourning in Santa Ana's finest hotel. Pake's instruction was for the gang to meet up in Roswell. Only then did Caleb realize that funds were substantially depleted. A quick count revealed only fifty bucks left. Following a consultation with his two buddies, it was found that Shifty Simms and Delta Jack were no better off.

So heading back up north into New Mexico was adjudged to be an unwelcome but necessary chore. That didn't stop the trio having some fun on the way though. Unfortunately, things had gotten out of hand in Elephant Butte. So here they were, tramping across this godforsaken wilderness with every chance they would not make Carrizozo on the far side.

'I'd give my cut of the next heist for a single canteen of water,' mumbled Delta Jack to nobody in particular. The others made no effort to take him up on the suggestion. They were all of a like mind.

But Lady Luck was about to step in with a helping hand.

It was the lead horse that smelt water. The roan's head lifted. It snickered, turning towards the source. Caleb immediately picked up on his mount's twitching ears.

'Well it's a good job you've spent it all.' His upbeat tone found the others lifting their bowed heads. 'Looks like the roan is trying to tell us something, ain't you gal?' the young tough burbled. A thick leathery tongue hindered his garbled croak. The animal's response was a hoarse yet buoyant whinny.

So he let the cayuse have its head. The re-energized horse picked up its pace to a shambling trot. No more than a hundred yards distant was a low outcropping of rock that protruded from the otherwise monotonous white carpet. They circled around to the far side.

And there it was, emerging from a crack in the rock wall. The rays of the afternoon sun caused it to glint like a cluster of diamonds. No more than a thin trickle, it was the nectar of the gods where thirsty men were concerned.

The outlaws hurriedly dismounted and threw themselves into the shallow pool at the base of the cliff. After slaking their thirst, they lay back on the sand, gasping for breath yet exhilarated. The horses needed no persuasion to fill their own bellies. Nobody moved for a long five minutes while the life-giving elixir coursed through their dehydrated bodies.

No dissent was voiced when Delta Jack proposed they make camp beside the pool. The water enabled a pot of strong coffee to be brewed. Celebration at their good fortune was further enhanced by the last of the finest hand-rolled Havana cigars. As for food, sticks of beef jerky would have to suffice until they reached civilization. Exhaustion soon claimed the bodies of the three owlhoots.

For the first time since entering the brutal wilderness of the White Sands they were all able to adopt the guise of the absent Ten Sleep. On previous nights, Caleb in particular had admitted suffering from nightmarish visions of being pecked clean by scavenging buzzards. No such problems during this night.

Yet it was one such predator that awoke them the next morning. The lone bird was circling overhead clearly assuming a hearty breakfast had come its way. Caleb snarled out a rabid curse and loosed off a couple of bullets at the startled creature. It flapped away in terror having lost a handful of feathers that drifted down to earth on the early morning thermals.

TWO

... TO WORSE

And so after five weary days, the notorious White Sands was finally left behind. Carrizozo was the first town on the far side. The cluster of wooden buildings had grown from a tented settlement of traders into a prosperous enclave due to its location on a crossroads. From here, trails radiated to the four points of the compass.

The Capitan saloon was their first port of call. One of half a dozen catering to the thirst quenching needs of passing travellers. Slapping the dust from trail-smeared duds, Caleb Ollinger led his buddies into the cool interior of the drinking den. Beers were ordered and downed in single draughts.

'Set 'em up again, bartender,' Ollinger ordered. 'Our mouths feel like they've been scoured out with sandpaper. And that ain't far from the truth.'

'You boys come over the White?' enquired Smiler Vaughn.

Caleb nodded, stroking the froth from his mouth.

'Never again,' butted in Shifty Simms. 'Hell and the Devil must be a paradise compared to that nightmare.'

'We only managed to cross safely because of a spring we found,' added Delta Jack.

'That must be Hondo Well,' Smiler informed them, effecting his cheery soubriquet. 'It was dubbed that by the guy who discovered it. You boys were lucky to have found it. Didn't you take along enough water for the crossing?'

'We had to leave … ' Jack was about to blurt out the truth of their hurried departure from Elephant Butte when a sharp toe jab on his leg from Ollinger cut short the careless outburst.

The kid speared his buddy with a malevolent glower. 'What my partner meant to say was that we found ourselves lost in the dark …'

Simms jumped in to pick up the thread. '… And before we knew it, the Sands had swallowed us up. Wandered around for days. But thankfully we made it across.' He then quickly changed the subject. 'Is there a poker game running at the moment? I feel like some action after trudging through all that white stuff.'

Vaughn slung a thumb towards a natty dude sitting in the corner who was idly playing patience. 'Black Spot is your man. He's our house dealer. And it looks like he's free.'

The gambler was wearing a grey derby. Beneath it sat an elegant waxed moustache, which the guy constantly twirled. Stuck in the hatband was an ace of clubs advertising his credentials. A yellow silk vest and brown checked pants effectively contributed to the gambler's persona.

The three men sat down at the table. Caleb slapped down the last of his dough. 'You ready to add to my pile, fella?' he sneered. As far as Caleb Ollinger was concerned, card wielders were a breed no better than the dirt on his boot heel. 'Cos we're feeling lucky, ain't we boys?'

The other two sniggered, dutifully setting down their own meagre wedge of dough.

'Always ready to oblige, boys,' the gambler replied. A frosty grin was pasted to his lean features as he quickly assessed these no-account drifters. Lowlifes who figured they could take him to the cleaners. But the wily gambler had their measure. 'Black Spot's the name, poker's my game,' he announced breezily while deft hands shuffled the pasteboards.

'Just deal the cards, smart ass,' snapped Caleb. 'And make sure there ain't no tricks pulled while you're at it.'

The gambler's face assumed a resentful demeanour. 'We always play an honest game in the Capitan. You gonna play or not?'

Caleb's snappy gesture of irritation saw the gambler flicking out the pasteboards.

The game progressed with both parties making little headway on the pot, although it soon became evident that Delta Jack and Shifty Simms were losing steadily.

After a half hour, with only a few dollars left, they both quit leaving Caleb the only one smiling. His pot had doubled. 'You guys need to take lessons from a master.' He aimed a cocky smirk at the gambler. 'Ain't that the case, Mr Black Spot?'

'You sure seem to know your way around a deck of cards, fella. Are you up to us raising the stakes?' A supercilious twist of the lip challenged this upstart to defend his showy bravado.

Caleb's arrogant sneer gave the gambler his expected answer. 'Why not? No limit, winner takes all. That OK with you?'

'That's my kinda thinking. So long as you don't mind losing.'

'We'll see who's gonna be laughing soon enough,' retorted the young braggart. He handed a wad of notes to Simms. 'You fellas go stock up on provisions while I skin this dude.'

Black Spot maintained a classic deadpan expression giving nothing away. As the two-handed game progressed, he allowed Caleb to win steadily. Then, an hour later, he made his play. Simms and Delta Jack had returned to the saloon just in time to observe the final play.

Caleb had bet his entire holding on this last hand. He called the gambler and laid down his cards. 'Beat that, mister. A full house, kings on jacks.' Clutching hands reached out to draw in the hefty pot, which by that time amounted to over 500 smackers. Only luck and the Devil could beat a hand like that. Greedy peepers fastened onto all that lovely dough.

Black Spot had timed his broadcast to perfection. 'Last I heard four of a kind beats your hand.' He laid down the quartet of queens. 'That means the house wins.' Now it was the gambler's turn to claw in the loot. 'Sorry, fella, you lost.' Spot's twisted grimace indicated that regret played no part in the outcome.

Just like his brother, Caleb Ollinger was a poor loser. His youthful features contorted. Eyes akin to red coals of fire glittered with menace. 'That ain't possible, Spotty. I saw that queen of hearts earlier in the game. You're a dirty cheating four-flusher.' For a brief instant nobody moved. You could hear a pin drop in the Capitan.

It was Caleb who broke the spell. His chair fell back as he grabbed for the revolver strapped to his right thigh.

The gambler was caught betwixt a rock and a hard place. He had no time to draw the pistol stuck in his vest pocket. A Colt .45 slug punched him back. A second made certain the guy had dealt his final hand. In moments, the saloon was in uproar as the three outlaws backed towards the front door. 'Anyone moves a muscle and it's the last time he ever will,' snarled Caleb, brandishing the shiny nickel-plated revolver.

Delta Jack and Shifty waved their own hardware to emphasize their intention to leave unmolested. But not without Caleb's alleged winnings. The kid scooped up the pot and stuffed it into the pocket of his fleece coat. Once outside on the street, they made sure that the saloon's clientele kept their heads down. A flurry of shots smashed through the front window. 'OK boys, reckon it's time we quit this berg.'

'Don't you think this is becoming kind of a bad habit, Caleb?' Simms grumbled as they mounted up.

'Quit your griping, Shifty,' the young tough admonished his sidekick. 'This sort of thing is what makes life exciting.'

The stocky bandit was a good fifteen years older than his headstrong young associate. In his glory days, Shifty Simms had been every bit as wild and carefree as Ollinger. But age had made him much more prudent, which included salting away a substantial part of his ill-gotten gains in a Santa Fe bank. One that was especially well guarded against the depredations of other guys in his profession.

His prime aim was to enjoy an early retirement before either hot lead or the law stepped in to sink his ambitions. Another year on the owlhooter trail should see him set up for life. Caleb's reckless bravado, however, was putting his plans in serious jeopardy. For now, however, it was yet another hurried exit that could easily have been avoided.

The younger Ollinger was totally oblivious to his older sidekick's reservations. His eyes glittered with something close to lunacy. He actually seemed to be enjoying life on a knife-edge. It was all part of the buzz when you were young and happy-go-lucky. Shifty could readily understand that. But it was no consolation for a guy of forty who knew he was living on borrowed time. Most road agents never reached anything near that.

'Ain't I right, Delta?' Caleb's leery grin received a burbled response.

'What's that you're saying, boss?' The slow-witted Jack was lost for words. All he wanted at that moment was to quit Carrizozo with his skin intact.

The three outlaws dug in their spurs and hurtled off up the street. Folks were scattered left and right as the reckless trio hammered up the middle of the street. So intent were they to escape retribution they failed to heed a young boy of around eight years who came dashing out of a side alley. He was chasing after a ball.

'Shooting up towns and getting the better of no-account tinhorns is all part of the fun.' Caleb's attention had switched to his sidekick rather than the way ahead.

It was Shifty who saw the imminent danger immediately ahead. 'Watch out for that kid!' he called out swerving his own mount to one side.

But Caleb merely laughed and ploughed onward. His mind was still preening over getting one over that cheating Black Spot. Before any of them knew what was happening the boy had been trampled under the pounding hoofs of the outlaw's horse. The boy didn't stand a chance. Simms chanced a look over his shoulder. The splayed out torso lay in the dust, unmoving.

'Goddamn it, Caleb!' he yammered out. 'Now you've done shot our bolt. Killing a tinhorn gambler is one thing, but a kid …' He shook his head in disgust. 'Them folks are gonna be mad as a nest of hornets.'

'I-I didn't see him,' whined the outlaw trying to play down his reckless act. 'The darned fool kid should have looked where he was going. It was a pure accident. Could have happened to any one of us. What d'you say, Delta?'

'Guess you're right there, Caleb,' the outlaw concurred, not wishing to brook the boss's younger kin. 'Must have been an accident.'

'Still don't make it right,' Simms persisted. 'Pake sure won't be too pleased at his brother running down a kid.'

'Then we won't tell him.' Caleb held his older associate with an intimidating glare before adding, 'Will we?'

Simms shrugged his shoulders. 'If'n you say so.'

'Good, then let's eat dust before those turkeys pick up our trail.'

Luck was on the side of the three fugitives. Bass McKendrick, the local tin star, was out of town accompanying the territorial governor on a visit to the neighbouring farmsteads. An election was due soon and the governor had every intention of being re-elected for a second term of office. Glad-handing was all part of the process.

THREE

TAKING A CHANCE

'I seen him,' Caleb growled out. His eye followed the pointing arm of Shifty Simms. 'He's been on our tail for some time.'

The three men were perched on the rim of a mesa overlooking the broken country to the east. It was on the third day out of Carrizozo that Caleb had spotted the telltale sign of rising dust to their rear. He had kept the unsettling discovery to himself figuring to out-ma-noeuvre what he assumed was a posse from the town. Only on this last day had he realized that their nemesis was nought but a lone rider.

They rode on, twisting between stands of rock, back-tracking and even erasing the prints of their horses in an effort to lose the guy. Nothing seemed to be working.

'We've tried every trick in the book to throw the bastard off,' grumbled Delta Jack. 'That guy is sticking to us like fleas on a dog's back.'

'Must be a bounty hunter,' Caleb declared. 'Those guys never give up once they smell a reward.'

'So what we gonna do?' Simms asked rather nervously. 'I was chased by one of them dudes up in Utah after robbing a stagecoach.'

'What happened?' Delta Jack was all ears to hear his buddy's explanation. 'Did you give him the slip?'

Simms heaved a regretful sigh. 'The sneaky rat caught me taking time out with a Ute squaw. I spent three years in the pen for that bit of pecker twitching.'

'Caught with your pants down, eh buddy?' sniggered Ollinger. 'I know the feeling.'

'More to the point,' Delta Jack cut in, 'what we gonna do about this fella? Pake ain't gonna like it.'

Caleb arrowed a caustic glower at the whinging speaker. 'Say that one more time and I'll swing for you.' The young tough's eyebrows then knitted together. 'I've been giving that some deep thought. And I reckon we should allow him to catch up.' The others looked aghast, regarding such a suggestion as ludicrous.

'Shouldn't we be putting some distance between us and a critter like that?' Simms averred with some dismay.

Caleb just grinned back. 'You guys ought to use your brains more.' He tapped his head knowingly then proceeded to outline his plan. 'Listen up and I'll tell you what we're gonna do.'

*

Chance Newcombe had ridden hard for Carrizozo after he received the wire from Marshal Wild Bass McKendrick. The boy who had been ridden down was the son of New Mexico's territorial governor. He and his family had been passing through the town on their way to Albuquerque for a meeting of supporters to discuss the forthcoming election.

McKendrick had known Newcombe from the days when they rode together during the war. The Gettysburg Green Hawks had since split up and gone their separate ways. While McKendrick had chosen the official path of law enforcement, his old partner had wavered between the right and wrong trails. He had finally opted for the dubious profession of the bounty hunter.

When the governor sought advice from Bass following the brutal death of his son, the marshal immediately thought of his old friend. Bass McKendrick's authority was limited to the immediate environs around Carrizozo. Last he had heard, Chance was operating out of Alamagordo, some three days' ride to the south. A wire was despatched to the local law officer to seek him out.

The shooting of the gambler known as Black Spot was of little account to the town marshal once he learnt that the guy had indeed been cheating. In effect, the three outlaws need never have left town in such a hurry. The law would have been lenient. Then this tragedy would never have happened.

That being said, other misdemeanours had since come to light after perusing the pile of wanted dodgers.

Caleb was the only one of the gang with a price on his head, albeit a small one compared to his brother Pake Ollinger. But the killing of a child was another matter. And when he was found to be the governor's son, stern action needed to be taken. Caleb's price was instantly doubled.

Chance had wasted no time in setting out to track down the killers. That was his job. A manhunter who hired out his gun to apprehend villains and outlaws beyond the remit of regular law-enforcement personnel. Dead or alive! That was the usual declaration plastered across the wanted dodgers gracing law office notice boards. Either option was acceptable to Chance Newcombe.

'A man draws his gun and takes his chance.'

That throwaway remark had led to McKendrick assigning the nickname that had stuck. And Jacob Newcombe was nothing if not fair-minded. He always offered his quarry the choice. And once embarked on a job, he saw it through to the fateful end. That reputation had made him the first choice for McKendrick when Governor Wallace sought justice for his dead son.

So here he was, five days out and confident of an early arrest.

A brisk nod assured the manhunter that he was following the right trail. Three sets of prints were a dead giveaway. It made him question whether these jaspers were careless, or merely over-confident. Smiler Vaughn, the bartender of the Capitan, had easily picked out the wanted poster of Caleb Ollinger from a pile in Bass McKendrick's office.

Newcombe was well aware of the Ollinger gang. They had been a thorn in his side for some time. Yet each time he had come close to nailing them, the critters had slipped through the net. Perhaps this time he would strike it lucky.

He already had a dodger for big brother, Pake. But that had now been discarded in favour of the latest one. An increased reward had been posted since the Flagstaff bank job in which a teller had been shot dead. That was in addition to the extra reward being offered by Governor Wallace.

But where the Ollinger gang were concerned, Chance Newcombe harboured a personal grievance in his quest of running them to earth. A reason that found him gritting his teeth at the thought that he might be close to finally laying it to rest.

He peered down at the clear prints beside a small creek where the outlaws had camped out the previous night. They led off in a straight line heading for the rising phalanx of the Cibola Mountains to the north-east. Chance was confident he would have these critters in the bag by nightfall.

He was entering the foothills, a meandering lab-yrinth of shallow draws and arroyos, when a plume of smoke up ahead caught his attention.

Dismounting, he tied off his horse and carefully edged his way up through the boulder field. The smoke, spiralling up like a twisted hank of rope in the static air was a homing beacon urging him onward. Closer and closer he crept, gun hand gripping the bone handle of his Remington revolver. Pausing on the far side of a large chunk of orange sandstone, he listened for any sound emanating from the supposed campsite.

Then a voice came to him from the rocky shelf. 'Come along in, stranger. The coffee's hot. I've been waiting on your arrival for a couple of hours. What kept you?' Chance didn't know it, but the invitation had come from Caleb Ollinger.

The sudden break in the silence took Chance by surprise. What game were these guys playing? Then it struck him. A clear trail had purposely been left for him to follow like a lamb to the slaughter. Before he was prepared to step out into the open, Chance addressed the speaker in a wary tone of voice.

'That's a tempting offer, fella,' he said. 'But how do I know you won't fill me with lead the moment I show myself?'

'You have the word of Caleb Ollinger on that,' declared the young tough. 'I just want to see who it is that's been following me. And for what reason.'

'Keep your hands where I can see them,' Chance ordered as he moved into view. 'And you're right. A man should know who it is that's taking him in to face the hangman. The name's Jake Newcombe. Some folks call me Chance 'cos I always offer a guy the choice.' He paused, a smile pulling down the side of his mouth.

'Live or die. So what's gonna be your'n?'

Ollinger was holding a mug in one hand and a coffee pot in the other. He nodded, holding out the mug. 'A bounty hunter. Yeh, I've heard of you. A real life tough guy, so they say. Here, take it. It's fresh made. And just so's you know, I don't have to make a choice.'

'And why's that?'

'You'll find out soon enough.'

'So where are your buddies?' the hunter demanded, reaching across for the proffered tin mug. 'I've been trailing three horsemen. Not that I'm particularly interested in the other turkeys. It's your brother I'm really after. But for the time being, you'll do. According to witnesses, you are the one that killed a boy and shot a gambler back in Carrizozo. And I aim to take you back to stand trial. That was the territorial governor's son and he ain't a happy man.'

Ollinger shrugged apathetically. 'I sent them on ahead while I waited for you.'

'And why would you do a fool thing like that?' Chance was watching the killer's every movement. He suspected what was in Caleb's mind.

'You'll never take me in, mister. Just thought I'd let you know, face to face.' The outlaw turned his head to one side and gave a perceptible nod.

That was the moment Chance lunged. He tossed the mug aside, grabbing hold of the outlaw's arm and spinning the critter round. His left arm circled the scrawny neck while the other hand jammed the gun barrel to the killer's head. A deep-throated roar echoed off the surrounding rock walls. The rifle bullet smashed into the rock behind where Chance had been standing moments before. It whined off into the void.

'Think I hadn't figured out your nasty little scam, buster,' he snarled, squeezing Caleb's windpipe. 'You better tell your buddies to hold their fire. Any more slugs come my way and I'll be taking you in strapped over a saddle.' Caleb struggled to free himself. But his eyes were glassing over as the airflow to his lungs was shut off. 'You hearing me, punk?'

A flaccid nod of the head saw Chance relaxing his hold. 'So tell them to back off,' he growled. The cocky braggart was left under no illusion that the hissed dictate in his ear was no idle threat.

Caleb breathed deep before calling out. 'He's gotten me buffaloed, guys. Don't shoot again else he'll kill me for sure.' But the prisoner was not about to be hauled off to jail without some show of resistance. One final attempt was punched out to shift the balance back into his favour. 'Go tell Pake what's happened. He'll know what to do. And tell him it's a bounty hunter called Newcombe.'

Chance waited until he saw the two owlhooters emerge from their cover in the rocks on the far side of the arroyo. He did not slacken his iron grip on the killer until sure they had departed. Then he threw Caleb down onto his stomach and slapped a pair of manacles onto his wrists.

'Might as well have some grub before we start back,' Chance declared, helping himself to a plate of wild turkey stew flavoured with oregano, cumin seeds and chilli powder. He was impressed. 'Boy, this ain't bad at all.' Ollinger scowled but remained silent. 'Where'd a no-account like you learn to cook?' The plate was soon empty as Chance mopped up the juice with a cornbread biscuit.

The kid was piqued at having his culinary expertise questioned. 'Just 'cos we rob banks and things don't mean we can't eat proper,' he retorted. 'My ma was head cook at the National Hotel in Denver. She passed on some tips of her best recipes afore they got rid of her.'

The puzzled look from the bounty hunter encouraged the kid to continue. 'A new manager took over. He figured a woman's place was in the home, not a hotel kitchen.' Caleb's lip curled with disdain as the foul memory returned. 'She was the main breadwinner of the family after my useless lump of a father drank himself to death. That was no great loss. But Ma losing her job sure was.'

Caleb was now in full flow. He had stolen a pistol from a sleeping lodger whom his mother was forced to take in to make ends meet. Then he went down to the National and shot the manager dead in front of a roomful of witnesses. After that he joined his brother who was already on the dodge for robbing a store in the town.

Both brothers had then fled west, losing their pursuers in the mountains.

As for their mother, she died soon after. 'The official line was that she caught the fever and never recovered. But I blame that skinflint of a hotel manager. She was never the same after losing the job she loved.' The life of the notorious Ollinger brothers on the wrong side of the law had, according to the brash young hard case, gone from strength to strength. 'That manager actually did us a favour. Ma would have been proud of us,' he finished with a swaggering flourish.

'Don't reckon any mother would be proud of a stuck-up piece of dung who rode down a helpless young boy,' Chance snapped. 'I have every sympathy for your ma. What she didn't deserve was to bring a cold-blooded thug like you into the world. And I'm gonna make certain you don't do it again.' He threw the plate aside and kicked sand over the embers of the campfire. 'Now on your feet. You have an appointment with the hanging tree.'

But Ollinger was not intimidated. He scowled back. 'Best watch your back, manhunter. Me and Pake stick together through thick and thin. He ain't gonna allow no trail bum to take me in for some neck stretcher to have his way. Your days are numbered, mister. So start counting down. 'Cos it won't be long afore they'll be measuring you up for a pine box.'

A stony look crossed Chance's face. Only a slight tic in his right eye betrayed a rising irritation with the kid's ranting invective. With little regard for any consideration, the outlaw was roughly manhandled onto his horse. 'Any more cussed jawing from you, fella, and I'll gag you. The choice is your'n.'

Caleb now saw the flinty regard in his captor's narrowed gaze and judged it prudent to haul in his mouth. For the time being at least.

FOUR

FRIEND OR FOE?

To avoid a surprise ambush from Pake Ollinger and his gang, Chance decided to take the longer route back to Carrizozo. It was across open flats but would entail an extra two days' travel. But should the desperado choose to attack, there would be plenty of warning to take cover. This route also had the advantage of their being able to stay a night at the Corona Relay Station.

Chance maintained a constant watch for any signs of his pursuers. The hunter's constant alertness was mockingly derided by his prisoner. On this particular occasion they were sat in the shade of some rocks.

'Don't matter how hard you try to avoid Pake,' Caleb sneered, puffing on a thin stogie his captor had permitted. 'He'll sniff us out and then toss you to the coyotes. But not before we have us a little fun.'

'What makes you think I want to throw him off the scent?' Chance replied with curt abruptness. During the day, he had deliberately slowed his pace as a plan began to form in his brain. But Ollinger was not listening. He continued to rant on about how his brother was going to deal with the bounty man when he caught up.

Chance took the invective for so long then lurched to his feet. 'I'm done warning you about trying to rile me, big mouth.' The hunter's patience had been stretched beyond breaking point. He grabbed the kid by the scruff of his neck and hauled him to his feet. A sharp backhander drew blood and a pained cry. Vehement protestations were to no avail. Chance wrapped the kid's necker around his yappy maw and tied it off. 'And for the rest of the day you'll be chewing dust.' He then heaved him over the saddle.

Minutes later they trundled off. It was a decidedly sore way to travel, not to say embarrassing. After an hour of the brutal treatment, Chance relented. 'Any more loose talk at my expense and you know what to expect,' he warned the sulking outlaw who quickly grasped the painful truth that words truly could hurt. 'You listening in, punk?' he snapped.

Caleb grunted something close to an affirmative.

It was around noon that they reached the relay station used by the overland stage line operating between Santa Rosa and Las Cruces. The journey across the dry plateau lands encompassed all manner of wild scenery. The contrasts were stark. Deep rocky canyons, barren and untamed with broken mesas, vied with grass-land where herds of cattle grazed contentedly. It usually took four days to complete the traverse with rest stations at specified intervals to provide respite for travellers.

The one at Corona was the most isolated, standing in the midst of an arid reach of sandy desert. It was the only place within a day's ride with its own well. Chance drew to a halt some hundred yards short of the adobe structure. A frown of concern creased his weathered countenance. It looked deserted. No horses, no signs of occupation. He loosened the revolver in its holster, nudging his horse forward at a slow walk.

Caleb likewise was peering around. He had hoped to find his brother already here. But that didn't appear to be the case.

Drawing closer to the eerie settlement, the door suddenly swung open and a man stepped outside. He was carrying a sawn-off and it was pointing Chance Newcombe's way. Behind him a thin spindle of a guy followed toting a lever-action Henry repeating rifle. Neither man was smiling. They just stood there, side by side as if waiting for the two approaching riders to come within range.

Caleb could see that neither of the men were members of the Ollinger gang. But they still raised his hopes of release. Any guys brandishing firearms at a bounty hunter had to be on his side of the fence. He let out a high-pitched yip of triumph.

'Yahoo! Seems like this is my lucky day, dude. Those guys don't look too pleased to see you. My guess is they're on the prod.'

A similar notion was passing through Chance's mind. They must have hidden their horses in the adjoining barn. Avoiding any sudden movement that might precipitate unwelcome retaliation, he continued to close with the relay station.

'Maybe I could join up with them until brother Pake arrives,' his prisoner prattled on. 'See what they're planning. Might be an extra bonus in it. Then it'll be curtains for you, bounty man. And I'll be first in line to fire the killing shot.'

Chance ignored the inane chirping. Fifty yards from the station, he drew rein. A narrow gaze focused on the first man, whose outline was now clearly defined.

He was a big guy with muscles bulging from his check shirt. Clean-shaven with curly black hair drooping from beneath the Texas high crown, which matched the hairy arms exposed to the elbows. His buddy had on a pair of buckskin pants held up by black suspenders over a dirty red one-piece. Bare headed, his lank blond hair reached down below his ears. Thin as whipcord was an apt description.

'No point in you thinking the Good Lord will come to your aid now,' Caleb niggled. 'These fellas have the drop on you. One wrong move and you're dog meat.'

The approaching riders hove to a halt outside the relay station.

'Soon as I saw that appaloosa, I figured it had to be you,' the big guy announced, lowering his shotgun. 'You always did favour that Idaho breed. But the army shirt was a dead giveaway.' The man coughed out what was intended as a laugh. 'Who except Jake Newcombe still wears one of them scratchy things after all this time.'

The bounty hunter leaned over the neck of his horse and nodded. 'Well I'll be darned. If'n it ain't Stag Bowdrie. I needed to get closer to make sure my peepers weren't playing tricks. Anyway, this piece of fine cloth keeps me warm of a night.' He shook his head in bewilderment. 'How long has it been, Stag?'

'Erm, now let me think … My reckoning is ten years.' The perky smile on Bowdrie's face quickly dissolved, being replaced by a less than welcoming pucker of doubt. 'And it weren't such a friendly parting if'n my memory serves me correctly.'

The thoughts of both men drifted back to when they had last rode together.

The year was 1866. Only twelve short months since the official termination of hostilities between north and south. Lee had signed the peace deal at Appomattox the previous spring. But many on the losing side were unwilling to accept defeat. Marauding gangs that had operated under the veiled legitimacy of war now found themselves on the wrong side of the new regime.

One such gang was known as the Gettysburg Green Hawks. Each man wore a green armband for identification. They were led by ex-lieutenant Jacob Newcombe, his second in command being Sergeant Staggert Bowdrie. Their targets were always northern supply columns. Half of the goods purloined by the gang were given to southern families who had been decimated by the brutal conflict.

The rest were sold and the profits split between members of the gang. The crunch came when Bowdrie took matters into his own hands and brought in an old associate who he reckoned would add some much needed bite to their activities. For some time he had been pushing for the gang to pull more audacious raids. Trains had been successfully robbed by the more renowned James gang. Why couldn't the Green Hawks enjoy a similar accolade?

Newcombe was wary and had vetoed the suggestion. He preferred to retain a measure of legitimacy to their actions. In his mind, they were keeping within the boundaries of lawful endeavour by helping their own kind regain their dignity.

It was inevitable that friction would follow. And the arrival of Mad Dog McGurk generated a confrontation that eventually led to the gang splitting up. McGurk had been a known bloodletter during the war. His brutal exploits were the equal of the notorious Bloody Bill Anderson who rode with Quantrill's Raiders.

Harsh words had been exchanged over McGurk's unexpected arrival. Some of the gang sided with Jake Newcombe. But most were with Bowdrie. Murmurings of discontent had been brewing for some time about having to share out their haul. Younger fellows who had had no involvement in the war were the most vociferous.

A split had inevitably followed. Chance knew that he

was at a break in the trail. One way led to a life on the run with lawless exploits booking that inevitable plot in some remote Boot Hill cemetery. On the other hand, he could change his ways, hold his head up high and follow a course of mundane, backbreaking toil as a dirt farmer.

Neither choice appealed. So he took the middle way and became a bounty hunter. Then he met the love of his life. And things changed almost overnight. But that was another story.

Eight years was a long time. Stag Bowdrie had aged somewhat. Track lines akin to the railroads he had robbed scored his leathery features. The black hair boasted more than its fair measure of silver threads. And the lean torso had spread to a more rounded shape.

But there was no denying he was still the ruggedly handsome dude that gals used to swoon over. The bounty man had heard about his adventures from time to time. They were mainly confined to the central plains states of Kansas, Nebraska and Missouri. As Newcombe had opted to move further west, their paths had never previously crossed.

Until now. It seemed like his old buddy had decided the pickings were much more lucrative west of the Pecos.

'You two guys acquainted?' Bowdrie's partner enquired jerking the two old comrades back to the present. Their dreamy preoccupation was of only a momentary duration when Whipcord Shorthand's jarring southern twang saw the two old friends visibly stiffening.

'You could say we were best buddies ... at one time,' came back the somewhat guarded response from the ex-sergeant. 'A few years before I teamed up with you, Whip. Meet Jacob Newcombe.'

'Most folks call me Chance now.'

'Don't tell me,' Bowdrie jumped in before his old pal could explain. 'You always give your targets the opportunity to surrender before shooting them.'

'How come you know about that?'

'Stands to reason.' Bowdrie slung a finger at the scowling outlaw. 'This guy is still drawing breath. Figure you gave him a chance to come quietly.'

'Ugh!' the bounty hunter grunted. 'Big mouth here talks too much. I had to hog tie and gag him to get some peace and quiet on the way here. As for the moniker, a marshal by the name of Bass McKendrick was the fella that coined it. You remember Bass? He's a town marshal over Carrizozo way.'

Bowdrie shrugged. 'I remember.' It was a less than complimentary endorsement of his old comrade's chosen profession. 'Never figured he'd go down that trail.'

The brief silence allowed Caleb Ollinger to butt in. His initial euphoria that a rescue was on the cards had faded. But now it brightened again after witnessing the tense stand-off. 'If'n you have a beef with this guy, I could help you out,' he posited eagerly to Bowdrie, hoping for the nod of approval. 'He's after taking me in to snatch a reward. Maybe we could join up. My brother is Pake Ollinger. Could be you've heard of him. He'd welcome a couple of eager gun hands to join our gang.'

Bowdrie swung his languid gaze towards the speaker. 'I agree with Chance here. You talk too much, mister.' The brittle gibe removed the smirk from Ollinger's face. His next remark was even less welcoming. 'And maybe I could take you in myself and claim the bounty.'

'I might have something to say about that,' Newcombe interjected. 'This guy's with me. And I'm taking him all the way.'

The two old comrades squared off, watching each other like hawks. It was Stag Bowdrie who broke the tense impasse with a conciliatory grin. 'Plenty of time for negotiations to take place,' he suggested. 'You and me have gotten some catching up to do. I've been hearing lots of tales regarding the exploits of Chance Newcombe the manhunter since we parted company.'

'All good I hope,' responded Chance accepting the olive branch. He had no wish to harbour grudges. But nonetheless, the hunter knew he would need to keep a wary eye on Stag Bowdrie and his oddball partner.

Bowdrie allowed himself a tight half smile. 'Depends how you look on them.'

Any further discussion regarding this unusual meeting was cut short by a sharply defined command from inside the station.

'If'n you guys have finished jawing, you can get moving. I don't want any of you hanging around Corona any longer.'

The icy stipulation belonged to a comely dame of middling years who now stepped into view. She stood in the open doorway, a work of art in contrast to the dark background. Chance couldn't help but run an appreciative gaze over the well-rounded contours, which, unlike Stag Bowdrie's, were all in the right places. The woman's flowing blonde tresses rippled in the desert breeze like ripe corn. Here was a vision to brighten up any drab landscape.

Equally eye-catching was the Spencer carbine clasped to her ample bosom. And it was clear that she was prepared to use it if necessary.

There could be no denying that Cara Lang was indeed a handsome woman. So where was her man? Surely this dame didn't operate a relay station on her ownsome. Chance didn't get the opportunity to question the woman who made her position clear as the crystal blue of her eyes.

'The weekly stage is due to call here soon and I don't want a bunch of gunslingers scaring off the passengers. This is a respectable halt and I intend to keep it that way. You're welcome to fill up your canteens from the well. Then I want you gone. And this hunk of iron will back my play.' The Spencer swung to cover the four unwelcome visitors. The hands firmly gripping the walnut stock did not waver.

'Looks like the lady is gonna have the final say, boys,' Caleb Ollinger chuckled.

Chance ignored the comment, shifting his gaze to

his old comrade. And it was chock full of disdain. Now he knew exactly why Stag and his partner had stopped off at Corona. They were intending to rob the stage and its passengers.

'You disappoint me, Stag,' he reproached his old buddy with a mournful shake of the head. 'Taking a woman hostage for your own ends.'

'It ain't what you think,' Bowdrie protested, reading his associate's mind. 'Me and my pard have other needs right now. And robbing the stage ain't one of them.'

Whipcord Shorthand slung a puzzled look towards his partner. A thin wisp of a guy, the skull-like head bobbled on narrow shoulders. The fella's gaping stare resembled that of a hungry coyote. And his thoughts were clearly in accord with those of the bounty hunter. 'What you saying, Stag? We ain't here for the stage?'

Bowdrie ignored the query. 'Things were getting a mite too hot for us up north. That's why we moved down here. To make a new start. But the only way I can shuck off the owlhooter yoke is by taking this dude in myself.'

Now it was Newcombe's turn to display a quizzical frown. 'What's your game then, Stag?'

'I guess you can't have heard. But the governor has issued a notice that anybody who brings in the killer of his son will be granted amnesty for all past crimes.' He paused, allowing the import of that revelation to sink in. 'You hear what I'm saying? It's gonna be me that takes Caleb in. That way I claim the reward and erase my dubious past activities. Me and Whip here will then have us a grub stake to start out with the slate wiped clean.'

The chiselled profile of the bounty man gave nothing away as he fixed his old pal with a look of solid ice. Silence reigned across the sandy wasteland as the two men faced each other. A long minute passed with not a word spoken. It was Chance who broke the deadlock. 'You'll have to go through me to do that, Stag. And I ain't for passing over my responsibility.'

Ollinger held his breath. Neither course of action suited him. His eyes twisted towards the east. That was the direction from which his brother ought to be coming. And the longer they stayed here, the more chance there was of Pake catching up.

'You guys hear what I say?' Cara Lang snapped out. 'Get yourselves out of here, pronto. I have paying guests to prepare for.'

The tense confrontation simmering in the desert heat was once again cut short by the interjection of Shorthand. 'And it looks like the stage is here now.' He pointed to the plume of ochre dust rising above the clumps of sagebrush.

All eyes swung towards the direction indicated. Moments later the Concord burst into view. And it soon became obvious that it was not for slowing down.

'What in thunderation is that driver doing?' Bowdrie ejaculated. 'He'll crash the darned coach racing like that.'

Charging hell for leather towards them, the gruesome reason for the Concord's panicky stampede stuck out like a sore thumb. Except in this case it was an Apache war lance skewering the driver to his seat like a butterfly pinned to a display board.

The team of six horses were careening across the flats, clearly frightened by the Indian attack on the coach. With no driver to direct them, the coach was totally out of control. And there could be passengers inside clinging on for dear life. It thundered past the station, churning up a miniature dust storm in its wake. A fatal crash was inevitable unless it could be stopped.

His once assertive presence as leader of the Green Hawks enabled Lieutenant Newcombe to assume control. 'Grab your horse, buddy. We have work to do.'

The quietly delivered directive of his old commander, brisk and decisive, was readily accepted. Sergeant Bowdrie needed no persuading. But he still had the wherewithal to give his partner firm instructions. 'Hey Whipcord, you keep this skunk under guard while we're away, yuh hear me?'

'Sure thing, Stag,' the lean beanpole asserted. 'He ain't going nowhere.' For the moment, the startling revelation concerning his partner's recent declaration was forgotten.

FIVE

RECOLLECTION AND RECRIMINATION

The two men then leaped on their horses and charged after the rampaging Concord. Side by side, ears bent back, their mounts needed no encouragement. They sensed the urgency of the chase.

'Seems like only yesterday, eh Lieutenant?' Bowdrie grinned. 'Remember that time on Marion Flats north of Wichita?'

'Could I ever forget?' Chance shouted across. 'Those freight wagons would have gone thundering over the gorge into Cottonwood Creek if'n we hadn't caught up with them in time.'

'Looks like we have the same problem here, buddy.' A hand pointed to the edge of a ravine up ahead.

'You know what to do, Stag.'

A brisk nod indicated there was no need for any explanations. Both men instinctively recognized the action that had to be taken. Bowdrie angled his horse to the left while Chance took the right. Slowly they drew level with the bouncing coach. A quick peak inside revealed there were three passengers. All were dead. Their bodies fatally punctured by arrows.

'When you're ready,' Bowdrie called out loud enough for his old friend to hear above the heavy thud of hoof beats.

'Let's go to it then,' was the immediate reply.

Chance judged his leap to perfection, grabbing a hold of the iron rail surrounding the upper luggage rack. His left boot heel found leverage in the open window. All his strength was needed to cling on before hauling his frame up onto the tethered pile of luggage.

The crawl across the top of the coach was fraught with danger. Swaying from side to side, the wild tilt of the unwieldy vehicle felt like a bucking bronco desperately seeking to unseat its irksome visitor. Chance hung on for dear life. He waited for the coach to steady before scrambling down onto the bench seat beside the dead driver.

His grizzly companion was difficult to ignore. But the main priority now was to get control of the wayward coach. A boot heel stamped down hard on the brake lever while clutching hands reached down to secure the flapping leathers.

Bowdrie meanwhile had spurred ahead until he was level with the lead horse. There he leaned across, awaiting his moment. Loosening his grip in the stirrups, he jumped onto the mustang's back, wrestling with the traces.

'You OK up there, buddy?' Chance called out dragging hard on the reins. The thin words were whipped away by the rush of dusty air. But Bowdrie acknowledged the concern with a raised hand.

The combined strength of both men was needed to rein in the cumbersome Concord. Chance tugged with all his might on the set of leathers, striving to wrestle the ungainly beast away from the inevitable plunge into oblivion. Up front, his partner-in-rescue made a similar manoeuvre dragging the head of the lead horse around to the right.

And they were only just in the nick of time. The coach rumbled and jolted to a bone-jarring halt. Steam rose from the flanks of the sweating team, their fear-choked eyes still flashing with terror. Muzzles snorted unable to comprehend that the nightmare was finally over.

The two saviours stepped down from their respective perches no more than three feet from the edge of the ravine. Gingerly they peered over the lip into the dark chasm. A sheer drop of over 200 feet met their startled gaze.

'That was too darned close for comfort, pal,' Bowdrie gasped out sucking in a deep lungful of air.

'I sure ain't about to disagree there, Stag. It feels like I've shaken hands with the scythe man himself. Much too darned close. But we made it.' Chance clapped his old pal on the back. 'Marion Flats don't come close to this baby.'

Bowdrie unwound his necker and clawed the sweat off his stubble-coated face. He slumped down on the hard ground. Chance joined him. Extracting a sack of Bull Durham, he rolled a couple of quirlies. Handing one to Stag, they lit up and drew in the soothing balm of the tobacco. For that brief moment at least they were old comrades once again, their recent stand-off forgotten.

It was Newcombe who broke the spell.

'I've always wondered why you brought in a skunk like McGurk,' he posited drawing smoke into his lungs. 'That guy was pure poison. At least before we operated with some degree of legitimacy. Bloody Bill Anderson and his kind brought the whole southern cause into disrepute. And rumour had it that McGurk was even more bloodthirsty.'

For a moment, Bowdrie was nonplussed by this unexpected challenge. But he soon recovered and expressed a spirited rejoinder.

'Didn't the James boys say the very same thing?' he countered stiffly in justification of their illicit deeds. 'Figured themselves to be a pair of latter-day Robin Hoods. But no matter how hard they tried to excuse their actions, in truth those guys were plain old robbers, just like us.' He offered his old pal a fixated regard seeking to force his view home. 'And thinking any different is living in a dream world.'

'But Mad Dog McGurk,' objected Newcombe, still unconvinced. 'At least we never deliberately shot anybody down. That guy was a sadistic screwball and proved it by living up to his name.'

'I ain't denying that,' Bowdrie admitted. 'Nor do I deny that I was also itching for more action. And more profit. Handing over half our loot was becoming a bone of contention. It all happened while you were away. Remember? That time you visited your folks back in Missouri?'

Newcombe gave a nod of recollection. 'I'd received a letter saying that Ma was dying of the fever and didn't have long to live.' His eyes watered as the painful memory was resurrected. He'd put Stag Bowdrie in charge of the Green Hawks until his return.

With the gang leader away visiting his folks in the town of Joplin, Bowdrie and the rest of the gang opted for a spot of relaxation in one of the new cow towns that were springing up in Kansas. Abilene was first choice. It had blossomed almost overnight at the end of the Chisholm Trail. A rip-roaring burg catering to the needs of Texas cowboys, it was ideal for a bunch of ne'er-do-wells with Confederate sympathies.

And in the late 1860s the law was not yet fully established. Gambling, girls and grog were readily available. Anything went in Abilene.

One night an old acquaintance made himself known to Bowdrie. The outlaw had briefly come into contact with Waco McGurk during the recent conflict betwixt north and south. And the guy's reputation for ruthless brutality was legendary. During the war such base methods had been viewed as a legitimate means of fighting.

Now it was over, Bowdrie naively assumed that the Mad Dog had been tamed. He still boasted that thick black beard, and three pistols were openly on display about his person. Had Bowdrie bothered to step outside and seen the scalps of victims tied to his saddle, he would have been far more wary of the newcomer.

The remaining members of the Green Hawks were sat round a table at the back of the Cow Palace Saloon when the hard-boiled tough planted himself in front of them.

'I hear tell you guys are looking for new recruits,' the Mad Dog declared fingering a .36 Navy Colt stuck in a cross-draw holster. 'The name's McGurk. I rode with Jersey Bob's Freelanders during the war. Maybe you've heard of me.' He gave the remark a brisk hoot of frosty laughter. 'It's not all true what they say, boys. Just the bad bits.'

The others joined in what they thought was a joke. But the flinty gleam in the newcomer's eyes should have given due warning that McGurk was no humourist.

'Who's in charge here?' the guy asked, pulling up a seat and helping himself to a slug of whiskey. Most of his features were hidden by a thatch of greasy black hair. The straggly beard was tied up with four red ribbons. Nobody laughed at the bizarre sight. Mad Dog was a description that fitted him like a glove.

'I am! And the name's Stag Bowdrie.' The reply was delivered with caution. 'Maybe you've heard of me. I rode with the Gettysburg Green Hawks. And I still do.' He threw a jaundiced look at the newcomer. This guy was too cocky by far. 'I don't know where you got your information, McGurk. But it ain't true. We don't need anyone else at the moment. Leave your credentials with my secretary here.' He slung a thumb at a little jasper known as Pinecone Adler. 'We'll let you know if'n a vacancy occurs. But I wouldn't hold your breath.'

The gang sniggered at the newcomer. But McGurk remained unfazed. He lit up a cigar and poured out another shot of whiskey. A lone gimlet eye held Bowdrie in a grip of steel. The other was covered by a black patch, one of many injuries the Mad Dog had acquired in the course of his depredations. They didn't seem to have hindered his arrogant self-assurance, nor a determination to have his own way.

Nobody talked down to him and escaped with a whole skin. But for now his ire was held back on a tight rein. He needed these critters.

'Maybe you'll be more accommodating when I tell you I have it on good authority that there's a bank not far from here loaded fit to bust with lovely greenbacks.' That piece of information certainly caught the gang's attention. As a man they leaned forward. 'Figured that might interest you.'

Bowdrie was sceptical. 'How come you know all about this?' he shot back.

McGurk tapped his pox-scarred snout. 'That's my secret. And I ain't spilling. All you guys need to know is that it's the real deal. Are you in or out? There's plenty more gangs around who'd snap my hand off for a chance like this.' His narrowed gaze panned the staring faces. A rabid smirk indicated he knew they had been well and truly hooked. 'But I'm giving you first refusal.'

'Me and the boys will need to talk this over,' Bowdrie decided after some thought. 'Go get yourself a drink at the bar.'

The deputy leader of the Green Hawks was highly sceptical of McGurk's bona fides. But the others easily over-ruled him. Stag Bowdrie was after all merely a stand-in for the more forceful Jake Newcombe. He signalled for the newcomer to return.

'OK, McGurk, you're in,' Bowdrie informed the newcomer reluctantly. 'So what's the plan?'

The bank of Abilene had been stockpiling dough supplied by a host of Chicago cattle buyers in anticipation of the large herds moving up the Chisholm from Texas. McGurk informed them that now was the time to go in there and snatch the lot. They would not get a better opportunity. But it needed a well-organized gang to succeed.

'You best be aware, mister, that we always split the take evenly and half goes to setting up southern families that lost everything in the war. You OK with that?' Bowdrie's challenge was clear.

McGurk shrugged. 'Suits me. There's enough in

that safe for us all.' He kept silent about his real intentions, which did not include any kind of magnanimous gesture. That was for weak-kneed mugs. But for now he would comply.

Bowdrie paused in his grim recollection of how Waco McGurk had infiltrated the Green Hawks. It was a harrowing reminder of a betrayal that did not sit well on his broad shoulders. He rubbed his hands, struggling to find the words to explain away how it had all gone wrong.

'You have a right to be angry at how I was taken in by the guy's persuasive blarney. McGurk might have been crazier than a loco mule, but he sure was a smooth talker. Had the guys eating out of his hand in no time. And I was suckered in with the rest of them. But at the time I had no idea that the infamous Mad Dog of legendary repute was still very much alive and kicking.' Bowdrie swallowed hard. His face blanched white before adding, 'Unlike the victims of that first raid.'

SIX

BITE OF THE MAD DOG

Newcombe had been listening quietly. His blank features gave nothing away. Nevertheless, he was totally enthralled by his associate's disclosure. 'So what happened?' he asked.

The raid on the Abilene bank had gone according to plan. All the money had been lifted. It was as they were backing out of the door that McGurk showed that his ruthless streak had merely been resting, awaiting an opportunity to be resurrected. He was the last out. The guy had deliberately arranged it that way. Two others were watching the street outside while holding the horses for a quick getaway.

Neither of the tellers nor the customers had caused the four members of the gang any trouble. It had always been the boast of the Green Hawks that no innocent bystanders had been killed during any of their illicit activities. Some had been wounded. Others who had resisted were clubbed down. Yet here was Mad Dog McGurk shooting two people dead for no apparent reason.

There was no time for protestations. Escape was their number one priority. And later when challenged by Bowdrie, the newcomer claimed the victims had drawn guns and he had been given no option. There was nobody to dispute the assertion. So it had been accepted as a necessary part of securing the handsome payday.

And there could be no denying that. It certainly was. Once the full extent of their haul was revealed, the shootings were conveniently forgotten.

Over the coming weeks, two more successful bank jobs were pulled off. The guy seemed to have an uncanny knack of knowing exactly where the most profitable heists could be initiated.

'I questioned him about it,' Bowdrie said puffing on his stogie, 'but he just shrugged and said it was a gift from the gods. I let it pass. The dough was flowing in and we were living the high life. Nor did I bother to enquire about the past associations of the people we robbed. It was only later I learned that McGurk made no distinctions between north and south in the targets he set up. That was around the time that you returned and we had that falling out.'

The bounty man's craggy features hardened at the recollection. 'I can remember like it was yesterday. We avoided a shootout by the skin of our teeth. You let that skunk have too much of his own way,' Chance grunted, admonishing the man he had placed in charge. 'You were supposed to be running the gang, not McGurk.'

'I admit it,' Bowdrie conceded, shamefaced. 'Like the others, I'd fallen under the guy's creepy influence. The rot had already set in. Afore I knew it, he was running the show.'

Both men sat for a spell, mulling over the what-might-have-beens. Following the fracas between them, Jacob Newcombe had left Kansas with a couple of loyal comrades and headed west, first into Colorado then down into New Mexico. Over the years that followed, the growing infamy of the Green Hawks passed him by.

Although disdainful of the failings divulged by Stag Bowdrie, Chance was nevertheless intrigued by the revelations so far divulged. He was also aware of his own shortcomings in not confronting the Mad Dog immediately on his return.

'Maybe it was my own fault,' he muttered in a downcast manner. 'I should have stuck around and had it out with the rat. But all I did was walk away. Wash my hands of the whole business. Maybe if'n McGurk hadn't been away himself sussing out one of those jobs, I would have. We'll never know.' He pondered for a moment on what might have been.

'And don't forget you took a couple of the guys with you,' Bowdrie added, firmly, reminding him of split.

Newcombe shrugged. 'We all went our own way. I ain't seen any of them since. So what happened after I left?' he asked, bringing the conflab back on track.

With Newcombe out of the picture, McGurk had

grabbed the opportunity to enhance his standing with the rest of the gang. He began to query why money was being passed onto folks that had done nothing to earn it. And he soon had the backing of the less altruistic members. At the same time, more victims were being shot dead. The Gettysburg Green Hawks had discarded their benevolent inclinations and become a common bunch of heartless desperadoes.

'It all came to a head when we arrived in Dodge City,' Bowdrie continued. 'The gang had grown to a total of eight. But we were beginning to divide up into two distinct factions. I knew deep down that the trail down which we were riding was wrong. And some of the other guys felt the same way. None of us were angels, but at least we had scruples, lines beyond which we would not stray. McGurk and his crew had no such limits. Far as they were concerned, anything that made a profit was fair game.' Bowdrie paused. 'You ever been to Dodge?' Chance shook his head.

'Boy, that was one hells-a-poppin' burg.' Bowdrie's eyes misted over at the recollection. 'Me and the others arrived first. McGurk was off on one of his cagey trips to suss out another money-spinning job. He always went off alone. I have to give the guy his due. That Mad Dog nose sure had the knack for sniffing out the best ones to hit.'

By 1872 Dodge City was booming. Cattle in their thousands were trundling north from Texas to the new rail head. Originally a meeting point for buffalo hunters, the town was given the humdrum handle of Buffalo City. It was only later that the presence of an army fort nearby commanded by a certain Colonel Dodge saw the name changed. The Postmaster General of Kansas claimed there were already too many places called Buffalo in the state.

As well as hunters, all manner of people flocked into the region. Not least in abundance were the whiskey pedlars, gamblers, soiled doves and gunslingers. The story has been told of a drunken cowpoke who boarded the train in Ellsworth and told the conductor, 'Take me to hell!'

'Get off the train at Dodge,' was the immediate reply.

And it was a pretty good description. Front Street was where it all happened. McGurk and his cronies were ensconced in the Long Branch saloon. Some of the Hawks were scared of the Mad Dog, but most latched onto his brazen manner and mysterious way of keeping them in the money. By this time Stag Bowdrie knew that he had made a grave error of judgement in taking McGurk on. Like a rabbit hypnotized by a swaying rattler, he had been hoodwinked by the guy's devious machinations.

There was only one way to make it right.

Four days passed as Bowdrie fretted over whether to make the challenge. With the backing of the other three men who were of a similar mind, he decided that the confrontation was inevitable. The quartet needed a few shots of whiskey in the Occidental to bolster their nerve for such a potentially fatal showdown. After checking their hardware, the men set off down the middle of

Front Street. It seemed like the longest walk of their lives as that date with destiny loomed ever closer.

As soon as they witnessed the grim procession, the regular citizens of Dodge knew that something was afoot. And as with many such incidents, it was likely to end in bloodshed. The street quickly cleared. In no time, only the four men were left. Although twitching curtains indicated they had attracted a morbidly curious audience.

Pausing outside the Long Branch, they spread out and hunkered down in readiness for the lethal encounter. On Bowdrie's right was Pinecone Adler with Shorty Dobbs to his left. Gully Nixx took up a slightly offset position. A quick check that his cohorts were ready, then he called out.

'I know you're skulking in the Long Branch, McGurk, and I'm here to tell you that your services are no longer required. Pack your gear and get out of Dodge pronto.' He was sweating buckets, but his hands were steady, hovering over the butts of his twin-rigged pair of .36 Cooper double-action revolvers. 'You hear me, McGurk?' he rapped out again. 'Get out here pronto and saddle up, or eat lead!'

Nothing happened for a good long minute. Neither the bark of a dog, nor the creak of a wagon wheel disturbed the tense silence. Then slowly, the batwing doors of the Long Branch swung outwards. The Mad Dog stepped out, an unlit cheroot stuck in the corner of his mouth. A leery smirk did nothing to encourage the challengers. The guy was far too damned sure of himself.

'I'm taking over this gang, Bowdrie,' he growled. 'You and your lily-livered cronies can take orders from me, or it'll be you what eats lead.'

'Think you can push me around?' Bowdrie shot back flexing his hands. 'This is a showdown. You know what to do. Now fill your hand and let's get to it.'

'I ain't packin',' the braggart scoffed, lifting his hands. 'You gonna shoot down an unarmed man?'

Bowdrie was puzzled. What devious trickery was this punk trying on?

'Now you drop your weapons.' McGurk's order was blunt and decisive. 'Or my boys know what to do. Best take a look on the roof tops to see that I ain't foolin'.'

The four men looked around and saw three rifles pointing their way. Too late Bowdrie realized that he had been suckered. This had been McGurk's intention all along. The Dog gave him no chance to decide one way or the other. Their fate was already determined. His arm dropped down. It was a signal for all hell to break loose. Gully Nixx was the first to go down. The others managed to draw their revolvers and make a spirited reply. But they stood no chance against long rifles. Powder smoke filled the street, hemmed in by the buildings.

In no time the echo of gunfire faded away leaving three dead men lying in the dirt. The battle of Front Street had lasted no more than thirty seconds.

Only Stag Bowdrie escaped uninjured. Luckily he was close to a wagon, which he immediately dived beneath as soon as the firing started. The drifting skeins now worked to his advantage. Seeing his close associates bite the dust one after another was a bitter pill to swallow. And it was typical of a conniving skunk like McGurk.

But personal recriminations would have to wait. For now a silent promise was hissed out. 'I'll find you, McGurk, and make you pay dearly for this. No matter how long it takes, my boys will be avenged.'

But first he needed to get away and live to fight another day. An ungainly backwards shuffle found him in the mouth of a dark alleyway. Assisted by the smoke, none of the assailants had spotted his covert manoeuvre. So he quickly scurried off to disappear between the two buildings and round the back of the amalgam of shacks and corrals behind the main thoroughfare.

There he hid in a barn until nightfall. Shouts from McGurk urging his men to dig out the missing challenger to his leadership claim came close. But nobody thought to search the dilapidated old barn. Once darkness had fallen, he crept out and secured his horse, leaving Dodge City far behind.

Once his associate had finished, Chance Newcombe sat awhile allowing the full measure of the disclosure to sink in. Revealing all that had happened was distinctly uncomfortable for Stag Bowdrie. Every word had been dragged from the very depths of his being. He just sat there staring out into the arid void. It was Newcombe who finally broke the awkward silence.

'So did you ever run the skunk to earth?'

Bowdrie lit up another smoke before answering. He

needed the calming influence of the tobacco to arrange his thoughts in order. 'Took me over a year before I managed to track him down. And that was a pure accident.' Newcombe was fascinated, despite his denigration of the guy's inept leadership abilities. 'I needed time to gather myself after that disastrous fiasco in Dodge. Don't mind admitting it. I'd lost my nerve. So I kept heading ever westward, as far from there as possible.'

Bowdrie had ended up in the mountain fastness of Cripple Creek, Colorado. That's where he had met up with Whipcord Shorthand. The two had hit it off right from the start. 'He's a simple kind of guy, don't ask nothing of me,' Bowdrie sighed wistfully. 'A total contrast to that asshole McGurk. And I'd trust him with my life. We make for a good team.'

With his confidence restored, Bowdrie was soon back to his old ways. The duo headed south-west into Arizona. And it was in Prescott that, out of the blue, he encountered his old nemesis.

The two buddies had been having a drink in Mulvaney's Bar. Whipcord had gone off to buy in some supplies. He had been gone a half hour when Bowdrie lifted his glass all set to finish his drink. It never touched his lips. For who had just walked through the door but his old enemy. The Mad Dog hadn't noticed him. He headed straight to the back of the room intent on joining a card game.

Bowdrie was momentarily taken aback at the sight of the cocksure braggart. His hand automatically reached down for one of the Coopers on his hip. Then he hesitated. Fear had suddenly paralyzed his frame. Now that the moment of confrontation was finally to hand, had his nerves failed him yet again?

Hate-filled eyes locked onto the odious snake's back. All the humble pie he had been forced to eat at the behest of this son-of-Satan flooded back into his mind. Blood surged through his veins. An angry snarl rumbled in his throat. There could only ever be one course of action to take, no matter what the outcome. He hitched up his gun belt, tossing back the rest of his drink.

Then he moved cat-like to the centre of the room. Wary eyes followed him. It was obvious to all those in the vicinity that lead was about to fly. Chairs quickly scraped back as men strove to remove themselves from the field of fire.

Bowdrie swallowed. His mouth felt dry. But he held his nerve. 'On your feet, McGurk,' he snapped out in a compelling tone that surprised even him. His hands flexed above both gun butts. 'We have unfinished business that needs sorting.'

For a moment the Mad Dog remained in his seat, even when the other card players dived out of the way. Then he swung around. A sneering twist of the lip was followed by a cutting insult. 'Well, well, if'n isn't my old pal, yellow-belly Bowdrie. Come to lick my boots, have you, chicken-liver?' The insulting jibes were meant to cower the challenger. In truth they did the opposite.

'Your days are numbered, crazy man,' Bowdrie hissed

back. 'Now cut the time wasting and slap leather. That is if'n you still have the nerve to take on someone face to face.'

The mocking leer was wiped from the brigand's face. He lurched to his feet and dragged out his pistol. At the same time, Bowdrie drew his. Both men fired at the same time. Shots were exchanged. Each of the participants was inextricably caught up in the tension of the moment. Yet despite the close range, none of the bullets hit their targets.

McGurk tried to concentrate his aim. But Bowdrie had skipped behind a pot-bellied stove. The slugs clanged off the iron shield. This gave Bowdrie the chance he needed. His next shot punched McGurk back. The varmint clutched at his left shoulder, seeking to trigger off another shot as he backed away.

But his assailant was now all fired up. He stepped out from behind the stove and was about to place his last bullet in the middle of the guy's forehead when his arm was knocked aside. The slug scored a furrow across McGurk's head. The single eye rolled up into his head, mouth falling open as he tumbled across a table.

Bowdrie swung round, angered at the interference with his quest for terminal vengeance. It was Prescott's town marshal Heck Davis who quickly wrenched the Coopers from his grasp. 'Good job I got here in time, fella,' the lawman said hustling his prisoner away, 'else you'd have been up on a murder charge.'

Somebody yelled for a doctor to come and see to the

wounded man.

'I was brought before a coroner's jury the next day,' Bowdrie finished off, 'but the verdict reached was that it had been a fair fight.'

There was nothing remarkable in this particular gun battle. But it had made front-page news in the local paper due to the number of bullets fired. Each of the participants had used two guns. It was regarded as a miracle that only woodwork and plaster had been harmed during the set-to. Even with all those slugs flying around, no innocent bystanders had been hit.

As a consequence, Bowdrie was released without charge.

'The marshal did advise us to leave town straight away though,' Bowdrie concluded with a laugh. 'Can't say that I blame him. Apparently, he had received word that the rest of the Green Hawks were camped out in a nearby canyon.'

'So McGurk is still on the loose?' Newcombe enquired.

Bowdrie nodded. 'Ain't seen hide nor hair of the jerk since that day. Maybe he's given up being such a bad ass and taken up dirt farming.' It was a hopeful suggestion to which neither man gave any credence. The skunk was out there somewhere, more than likely thirsting to get even.

Once more, the duo sunk back into their respective musings

SEVEN

NIGHT WATCH

All too soon the moment of peaceful reflection was over. Chance looked at his old pal. His next words were measured, flat and devoid of emotion. 'Don't think for one moment that telling me all this is gonna change anything. Caleb Ollinger is going back to Carrizozo to stand trial. And it'll be me what delivers him.'

Bowdrie held the other man's gaze. 'Guess we both know where we stand then.'

'Guess we do at that,' Chance declared, standing up and stretching his stiff frame. 'Now let's get back to the station pronto.' With that in mind, he climbed back onto the coach and tugged the war lance from the driver's body. 'Them Mescaleros are likely to be still around here wanting to finish the job.'

'A bit far north of their regular hunting grounds, aren't they?' Bowdrie offered while he studied the Apache markings curled around the shaft. He knew that any personal wrangling with Newcombe had to be set aside in order to overcome their current difficulties.

'Could be they're after the horses kept at the relay station,' the hunter suggested. 'There weren't any in the corral. And these places always have a dozen or more for the changeover when the stage passes through.'

Bowdrie nodded, sticking his head inside the passenger compartment. He quickly removed it, clapping a hand to his nose. 'Three dead men in there and they're starting to reek some'n awful. Best we get back and organize the burial.'

The short ride back to the station was conducted in silence. Each man's thoughts reverted back to their uncomfortable friction with regard to the prisoner. Neither was about to give way. And there could only ever be one outcome. What that would be was now in the lap of the gods.

Caleb Ollinger was none too pleased at being made to break sweat digging the four graves. The rant of displeasure was received with stoic indifference by Chance Newcombe. He allowed the cocky strutter to have his say, then merely stood in front of him and drew his pistol.

'You have a choice here, Caleb,' he mouthed, effecting a blank expression. 'Either dig four holes, or just one for yourself.' The equanimity of the blunt warning made it all the more poignant.

Whipcord Shorthorn howled with glee slapping his thigh. 'Yessir, I like it. That sure is a good one, Mr Newcombe.' Dancing around in front of the manacled captive, he couldn't resist a bit of owlhoot baiting. 'So what's it to be, kid-killer? A bit of sweat or a hunk of lead? I ain't too bothered about the state of your health, but I know who will be digging them graves if'n you choose wrong.'

Caleb scowled. 'OK, give me the spade,' he snarled. 'You critters will come to regret treating me like a slave labourer. Pake will have heard what happened by now. And he won't take kindly to me being treated like this.'

Trying to assume his most intimidating pose, he held out his hands for Chance to unlock the cuffs. Once released, he snatched up the spade. For a brief instant he toyed with the foolhardy notion of using it as a weapon.

'Try it, asshole, and Whipcord here will be a mite displeased at having to dig four holes.' The cocked Remington backed up the hunter's pledge.

The icy threat knocked the stuffing out of Ollinger's braggadocio. He knew when he was licked. But that didn't stop the outlaw growling like an ill-treated dog as he began hacking at the hard ground. Satisfied that no further action was necessary, the three men took their ease in the shade of the station veranda assisted by some cool lemonade prepared by Mrs Lang.

They were also looking forward to sampling a bit of home cooking, the smell of which was wafting through the open window. With the stage passengers having lost their appetites, there was all the more for them. As Whipcord Shorthand was not slow in informing his associates. 'My belly's rumbling like a thunderbolt. Guess we'll be able to have second helpings now.'

Cara Lang was taken aback by the laid-back attitude adopted by these men following the shocking events. But she recognized that with rampaging Indians around she needed them until her husband returned.

'How come a woman like you is living out here all alone, Mrs Lang?' Chance enquired, sipping his drink. 'This is dangerous country. There's enough proof of that right over yonder.' A languid hand pointed at the four covered bodies.

'Our horses got loose from the corral,' she replied through the open window while preparing the meal. 'Tom went out looking for them. That was two days ago.'

Chance arrowed a knowing look at his old partner.

'If'n you were my woman, I sure wouldn't leave you stuck out in this isolated spot, especially with Apaches sniffing around. The guy must be either running scared or a darned fool.'

Cara bristled with indignation at the effrontery of the thoughtless remark. She stamped out of the station and stood in front of him. Hands on hips, she aimed a bitter scowl at the speaker, paused for a moment, then stepped forward. Her arm rose with the intention of slapping him in the kisser. A hand shot up to catch the swinging blow before it landed.

That made her even more annoyed as she pulled free. 'How dare you come here accepting my hospitality then call my husband's loyalty into question? He's more of a man than any of you will ever be.' She turned to storm off back into the station. 'Tom will be back soon. You'll see. And he won't take kindly to insolent varmints like you still hanging around.'

Chance was taken aback by this woman's reaction to his tactless comment. But he had never been one to allow opinions of others to bother him. Even a comely dame like Cara Lang. 'If'n you weren't so feisty and stopped to think, ma'am, you'd have realized that it's the Apaches that have likely stolen your horses. So I don't hold much hope of you seeing the guy again in one piece.'

Tears flooded the woman's eyes. A hand rose to cover her chagrin before she disappeared back into the station.

A series of admonishing sighs to his left found the bounty hunter's face reddening. The notion was dawning that he had gone too far.

'You never did have much luck with the ladies did you, Chance?' Bowdrie scoffed with a sardonic shake of the head. 'Now I can see why. The last thing a woman needs at a time like this is her allegiance being questioned by a stranger. Then him adding fuel to the fire by telling her she ain't gonna see the guy again.'

'Maybe I did spout off,' Chance conceded. 'But I was just saying it as it is.'

'What you need, old buddy, are lessons in how to woo a dame properly.' The boasting Lothario jabbed a thumb into his chest. 'And Stag Bowdrie is the man to see you right on that score. But not with her. Old Whip here has more chance in that department than you.'

'I didn't do so bad in Tucson,' the skinny dude remonstrated. 'Red Sally sure gave me the works. Boy, was she some'n else. What she couldn't do with them tasty lips of hers ain't worth the telling. She even ...'

'We don't need to know the gory details, fella,' Chance butted in, curtailing Whipcord's erotic visions.

Bowdrie scoffed. 'And she made you pay three times the going rate.' He then turned his attention back to the discomfited bounty hunter. 'Anyway, as I was saying ...'

'If'n I ever want advice about women, I sure won't come running to you,' Newcombe interposed once again, fixing a jaundiced eye on his old pal. 'Remember Maisy Lovelace? I can see it all now, just like it was yesterday. Her angry husband chasing you down Ellsworth's main street with your pants flapping round your knees. That sure was some sight to behold.'

'You never told me about that,' Whipcord perked up, stifling a bout of chuckling.

'A man don't want such things bandying around,' Chance cut in with a wry smirk, glad to shift the awkward conflab away from his own failings. 'Ain't that so, Stag?'

'Guess I asked for that,' Bowdrie acknowledged, accepting the joshing in good part. Then he quickly brought the matter of their current predicament back into focus. 'So what are we gonna do about these Apaches?' His narrowed gaze panned across the bleak expanse of rolling terrain. 'They're out there some-where. Just waiting on a chance to come in here and finish us off.'

'What makes you think they'll stick around?' Whipcord asked.

His partner nodded towards the line of hills to the west. 'See that smoke?' Whip nodded. 'It's calling for a pow-wow. The critters who attacked the stage were just a small hunting party. My bet is they're after gathering strength in numbers.'

'Just looks like a regular fire to me,' Shorthand mut-tered, unconvinced.

'That's 'cos you ain't got the know-how, fella,' the manhunter said in agreement with his old pal. Chance was equally keen to shift his thoughts back to the task in hand. 'Reading Indian sign saved our bacon more than once. Stag's right. So we'll stay here overnight, then set off first thing in the morning.'

'What about the woman?' asked Bowdrie, who had been casting an appreciative eye over Cara Lang's willowy contours. 'She won't want to leave here if'n she still thinks there's a possibility of her husband returning.'

Newcombe's rejoinder was issued in a subdued whisper. 'You know as well as I do that those Apaches have likely finished him off. So she comes with us. In the meantime, we'll take turns to keep watch through the night.'

'I heard tell that Indians won't attack after dark.' Whipcord's suggestion was met with derisive grunts from both his older associates.

But it was Bowdrie who voiced their joint opinion. 'Some do, some don't. But I for one ain't for taking the chance of having my hair lifted while I'm asleep.'

It was a couple of hours later that the three men were once again sat on the veranda watching the sun disappear over the western horizon. 'That was mighty good cooking, ma'am,' Bowdrie complimented the woman.

Whipcord gave a vigorous nod of accord. 'Ain't had vittles that good since I don't know when.'

Chance Newcombe merely grunted. 'I'll take first watch,' he declared. 'You can relieve me around midnight.'

Bowdrie nodded. 'We'd best get some sleep, Whip. Looks like it's going to be a long night. The barn has some dry hay. That should suit us fine.'

Ollinger was chained to an outside fence post. His griping went unheeded.

After settling down in the barn, Whipcord was soon snoring happily. Bowdrie envied the simple guy his ability to shelve problems at the drop of a hat. He himself found it impossible to shuck the delicate situation into which they had stumbled. For a while he lay there staring up at the velvet canopy through an open window, marvelling at its star-spangled pattern.

Chance Newcombe was the fly in the ointment regarding his plans for Caleb Ollinger. Only that stubborn-willed bounty hunter stood between him and the new life he craved. Sooner or later a confrontation between them would be inevitable. Much as he regretted it, the guy was heading for an early grave. Cara Lang also kept intruding on his thoughts. But that he didn't mind a jot.

He eventually fell asleep. As a man constantly on his guard, Stag Bowdrie was a light sleeper. Perhaps when he'd taken Ollinger in and secured that vital amnesty, a proper night's rest would be possible. Until then, cat-napping would have to suffice.

He was thus able to spell Newcombe at the appointed hour.

Standing behind the lone sentinel, his hand tightened on the Henry. One shot, that's all it would take. He couldn't miss. And nobody would know what had happened. Just a shot in the dark, ostensibly from those loitering Apaches, and it would all be over. The broad back of his old friend made for a solid target. Go on, get it over with. You owe yourself a fresh start. The devil was perched on his shoulder, wheedling and cajoling, egging him on to finish the job.

'You gonna pull that trigger, or not?' Newcombe slowly turned around. His old pard looked abashed, like a kid caught with his fingers in the cookie jar. Shame at even contemplating such a heinous act was written across Bowdrie's face. The other man made no attempt to raise his own gun. It was as if he had known all along that Stag would not be able to live with himself if'n he had gone ahead and hauled off. 'I figured not,' he said in a soft understanding ululation. 'That sort of lowdown dry-gulching is for the Caleb Ollingers of this world. Guys like us do the job properly, man to man.'

The challenge was there. Unspoken yet clear as mountain dew.

Bowdrie attempted to shrug off the notion. 'The thought never crossed my mind.' But it was a weak denial. And his old pal knew it. The moon's ethereal glow illuminated a face cloaked in guilt. He also knew, like Bowdrie, that sometime in the none too distant future, there would have to be a showdown.

A cough to hide Bowdrie's discomfiture brought the conversation back to the matter in hand. 'Any signs of them red devils?' he posited, joining his associate.

Newcombe allowed the uncomfortable moment to pass. And together the wary comrades peered out into a murky void.

'Only the usual giveaways, you know – owl hoots and coyote yelps. They're still out there all right. Like as not they know we'll be watching, and waiting.'

'You get some sleep. Whip can follow me and wake us at the right time.'

A look born of shared hardships and dangers overcome passed between the two men. For the moment they were linked to the common cause of coming through their current predicament unscathed. After that when the chips were down, who could say which way the ball would roll.

'See you in the morning, buddy,' the hunter said, moving away. Bowdrie smiled to himself. It was an unspoken accord that bound them together whatever the future might hold. Should it come to a showdown at some point in the days ahead, both men would face it with their heads held high. No recriminations, no animosity.

But only one would walk away.

'Yeh, sleep well, buddy.' Newcombe lifted an arm to show he had heard. Bowdrie paused before adding, 'You might not have many more left to enjoy.' But the muttered postscript was heard only by the night air. Chance Newcombe had gone.

It was sometime around the middle of his watch that Bowdrie sensed the presence of Cara Lang by his shoulder. It was her smell. A musky bouquet that only a woman could exude. And it stirred his loins.

'Can't you sleep either?' he said, without turning round.

She handed him a mug of coffee. 'It's not easy with those red devils out there, just itching to come in here and finish us off.'

Side by side they stared out into the pitch-black void. The lantern normally left outside the way station to guide late-arriving travellers had been doused. No sense in asking for trouble. Such a beacon would attract more than moths to the flame, in the form of Apache arrows.

The sounds of night-time in the wilderness filtered back across the emptiness. It could have been a peaceful setting in other circumstances. Although at that moment, it was the tingling presence of Cara Lang that was uppermost in Stag Bowdrie's thoughts. In answer to her query, he nodded. Then hawking out a brief guffaw to disguise his licentious thoughts added, 'I always envy Whipcord. That guy can sleep through a thunderstorm.'

He continued to stare out into the inky blackness. The unwelcome Apache presence turned it into a sinister place with every dark silhouette assuming the form of an enemy waiting to pounce. Yet with this woman by his side, for once in his violent life, Stag Bowdrie felt at peace with himself. If'n she could somehow be persuaded to share his life, the forthcoming amnesty would be nothing short of perfect.

But such musings served no purpose. It was all a fantasy, an idle reverie invented by an overactive imagination. It was Cara who innocently broke in on the fantasy pipe dream.

'Your friend the bounty hunter seems to be a very lonely sort of character,' she commented. 'He acts like he don't want anybody to get too close. The guy hasn't even cracked the hint of smile since he's been at Corona. I'd say he's toting a massive grudge against the world. And it's made him hard and distant. Like something happened in his past, something bad.' She paused to see if her companion would elucidate.

All he said was, 'You ain't too far from the truth there, Mrs Lang.'

She waited for her companion to explain. But he remained tight-lipped. 'Well? Are you going to tell me what happened?'

'I don't know all the facts. All I can say is that

according to rumours it couldn't have been much worse.' Now it was Bowdrie's turn to stand aloof. He clammed up. A man's personal business was his own affair. And he proceeded to make that abundantly clear. This was one point beyond which no man worth his salt would stray. 'I've said too much already. If'n Chance wants to explain, he'll do it in his own good time. Even if'n I'd known, it ain't my place to disclose a guy's deepest heartache.' He turned to face the woman. 'And he wouldn't thank you for asking either.'

'I didn't mean to pry,' she apologized, conscious that she had strayed into territory best left alone.

Bowdrie offered her a mollifying smile. 'I know you didn't, ma'am. But I have to agree with him on one point.' Her raised eyebrows encouraged him to continue. 'A man has no business leaving his wife alone in this country.'

Somewhat piqued, she retorted, 'I can look after myself.'

'I'm sure you can. Still don't make it right.'

'No need to fret, Mr Bowdrie,' she said in a frostily restrained tone of voice. 'Tom will be back tomorrow with those runaway horses. You see if'n I ain't right. Then you and your associates can be on your way. In the meantime, enjoy your coffee. I'm sure those Indians will have departed when day breaks.'

And with that final comment, she left him.

'I doubt that, ma'am,' he murmured under his breath. 'I doubt it very much.'

EIGHT

FAIR EXCHANGE?

They were up next morning at the crack of dawn. Following an early breakfast of fried eggs and bacon washed down with strong coffee, even Caleb was forced to acknowledge the woman's culinary expertise. Cara had reluctantly agreed to accompany them to the next way station, some fifteen miles to the south-west, seeing as her husband had not returned.

Newcombe was out front busily organizing their imminent departure.

'I expect we'll meet Tom along the way,' she said while packing her own belongings in readiness for the journey.

He gave the remark a world-weary sigh but held his peace while tightening the cinch strap on his saddle.

Over by the corral, the searching eyes of Caleb Ollinger panned the harsh landscape hoping for his brother to make an appearance. But all he found was a line of Apache warriors. Dark silhouettes atop a ridge, sinister and menacing, etched starkly against the orange backdrop of the eastern skyline.

'We got company,' he called out in a less than ecstatic voice.

The others paused in their allotted tasks and followed his pointing arm. As if in answer to the warning, three of the leading bucks detached themselves from the rest and rode down from their lofty perch. They stopped a hundred yards from the station.

'Looks like they want to talk,' Newcombe observed.

'What do you reckon they want?' was Whipcord's tremulous query.

'Only one way to find out.'

He swung into the saddle and moved off at a steady gait so as not to alarm the redskins. None of the watchers could hear the verbal exchange, which was accompanied by various gestures and hand signals. Five minutes later the bounty hunter was back.

'Are they after more horses?' Bowdrie asked. 'We can give them those from the stage team.'

'It ain't that,' replied Newcombe, sucking in a breath. 'The leader is called Hachita. Says he's seen the woman and wants her for his lodge. I told her she was too skinny and bad-tempered for Apache tastes.' Cara Lang's hackles rose as she gave him a sour look. It was ignored. 'He wants her in exchange for allowing us to have a free ride out of here.'

Newcombe gestured for the woman to mount up.

'You ain't giving her away, are you?' protested Bowdrie, stepping in front of the woman. His hand rested on the butt of his revolver. 'I sure ain't for that.'

'Neither am I,' came back the shrugged reply, 'but its best we play along and I try to persuade them that horses are more valuable. You guys keep us covered. That Hachita didn't look like he was the negotiating type. So we might have to make a quick departure.'

'I hope you know what you're doing.' Bowdrie's proviso was restrained. 'Those guys are getting a mite too close for comfort.'

It was true. The Apaches had steadily moved up to within a stone's throw of the station. They made for a distinctly uncomfortable presence.

'So do I, buddy, so do I. All I know is that most Apaches value horses above anything else. Let's hope this guy does as well.'

And with that he and Cara walked towards the waiting line of Indians. 'Don't make any sudden moves,' the bounty hunter advised the woman. 'Just stay calm and let me do the talking. These fellas don't take kindly to a woman displaying her emotions. They take it as an insult.'

Seeing the two people approaching, the Mescalero chief assumed there was to be a trade-off. He called for one of his men to bring up a horse. That was like pouring water on hot fat. Newcombe was given no opportunity to plead his case. Cara screamed, clapping her hands to her mouth. She turned away, her body visibly shaking.

Any semblance of calm had been dissipated. The Indian ponies skittered and jumped about at this sudden outburst. One brave lifted his war lance ready to throw it. The white man had little choice but to draw his gun and shoot the assailant.

'Get back to the station!' he yelled out, backing away himself while keeping the Indians covered. Another couple of shots over their heads urged the angry bucks into retreat. 'It's lucky for us that only three have chosen to come down here.'

Bowdrie and his pard gave them covering fire from the safety of the encircling stone wall surrounding the station compound. The Indians rode back to their comrades on the ridge. But Hachita was no fool. He knew that to make a frontal attack would invite death from the white eyes' fire sticks. Instead he held off, knowing that time was on his side.

'What in blue blazes is wrong with you, woman?' Newcombe railed at the distraught female. 'Didn't I tell you to keep a cool head? Now you've really gone and upset the apple cart.' He knew that Mescalero Apaches were tenacious fighters who would pursue their quarry until vengeance was attained.

'You want to know why I'm so upset?' Cara was struggling to keep herself under control. 'That was my husband's horse they brought up. That's why, Mr High-and-Mighty bounty killer.'

'Well we can't stay here now,' Newcombe declared, feeling like a heel but still not prepared to apologize.

'Get your things together. The rest of you mount up. We need to reach the next station before sundown.'

Cara Lang offered no resistance in accompanying the group to the Del Macho way station. Accepting that her husband was dead had knocked the fight out of her.

Throughout the journey to Del Macho, Whipcord Shorthand kept a constant watch on the horizon for signs of the Mescaleros. He was decidedly nervous. And not only because of the Indian presence. Pake Ollinger and his gang were also on their trail. The route took them across open flats with precious little cover should they be attacked. Newcombe on the other hand appeared unconcerned.

Whipcord voiced his anxiety to his pard. 'That guy don't seem bothered about us keeping close to the foothills where there's plenty of rock cover.'

'I'm more bothered about the rest of the Ollinger gang catching up and snatching Caleb,' Bowdrie hissed. 'We can keep those Indians at bay with our guns. But Ollinger is bound to have the latest repeaters.' Then another thought struck him. 'But you're right about him keeping us in the open. The guy don't seem bothered about us upping our pace neither.'

'What's his game, d'yuh reckon?'

'Looks to me almost as if he wants that gang to catch us.'

'That's plumb crazy,' exclaimed Whipcord. 'Why would a guy want to do that? Don't make no sense.'

'It sure is a mystery. Some'n is bugging him,' Bowdrie speculated, his cynical regard prodding the back of his old buddy who was leading the way. Then a thought struck him. 'And I have a hunch that I know what it is.'

'Don't matter none what he's up to,' Whipcord grumbled. 'It's Ollinger and his gang that's putting the frighteners on me, Stag. Why don't we just pull out and leave Caleb for Newcombe? Let him keep the reward. He might not even reach Carrizozo if'n Pake puts a bullet in his guts. That could be our reward as well if'n we choose to stick around.'

Bowdrie shook his head. He was adamant. 'I ain't leaving without Caleb. It's the amnesty I want. He's our ticket to a better life. And I ain't scared of Pake Ollinger neither. If'n he wants to rescue his brother, the three of us are equal to the challenge. And that includes you if'n you still want to ride with me when this fracas is over.'

'I ain't no milksop, Stag,' the beanpole remonstrated. 'You should know that by now. Course I'm staying. Ain't I always proved my worth?'

'Just telling you how it is, Whip,' Bowdrie placated his buddy. 'I know you meant well. But if'n Pake don't arrive soon, Chance will have to face me. Either way, he's hit a losing streak.'

Before Bowdrie could expand further on the gritty issue, a shout from up front saw them all turn to follow Newcombe's pointing hand. The line of Apaches was trailing them on a parallel ridge. And they were all painted up.

Whipcord sighed. He was not a follower of religion. But now he crossed himself. Here was yet another problem he could have done without. A miracle would be needed for them to come out of this fracas in one piece. Even if'n he had wanted to abandon his partner and save his own skin, that option had now been removed.

It was obvious the Indians were intent on a vengeful confrontation. Worst of all, during the intervening period, they had been joined by others with rifles. These were clearly visible and intended to strike fear into the hated white eyes. They were being successful in that respect.

Newcombe had reined his horse to a halt, allowing the others to catch up.

'Mrs Lang here tells me the Del Macho station is on the far side of that ridge. On our present course those redskins are going to cut us off before we reach it. But she knows of an old adobe trading post further down this arroyo. It was abandoned some years ago but will offer us a place to shelter.'

The woman now added her knowledge to the discussion. 'Once the Overland started up, the new Del Macho relay station made the one down here at Artesia unnecessary. All trade passed them by. Josiah Briggs and his wife carried on for a spell. But the new route had cut them off. Nobody came this way anymore. Last I heard they had gone back east to Kansas City.'

For the next few minutes they trotted along in line

making no attempt to flee the imminent threat. The Indians maintained the same pace on a parallel course.

'Them Mescaleros look to me like they're ready for action,' remarked the tremulous voice of Whipcord Shorthand. The others could only agree as the band of renegades suddenly came surging down the slope. Yipping and hollering, it was clear they had scalp hunting in mind.

'How far is this old station?' asked Newcombe as they spurred off.

'Just over the brow of that hill,' replied the woman. 'Ten minutes at the most if'n we push the horses.'

'You go ahead while me and Stag here try to stall them.' He pulled a rifle out of the saddle boot and pumped a couple of shots in the direction of the charging Apaches. Bowdrie joined him and added his firepower to the delaying tactics. It appeared to have the desired effect of stalling the Indian rush. Nevertheless, it could only ever be a temporary reprieve. Hachita swerved away, leading his warriors in a looping move away from the line of fire.

The respite had, however, afforded them valuable time to reach the shelter of the old Briggs station.

'That guy Hachita must be awful keen to add the dame to his lodge,' the bounty hunter remarked acidly as they galloped towards the broken-down old station.

'Can't say that I blame the guy,' remarked Bowdrie, riding alongside him. 'I sure wouldn't mind risking a fracas for a woman like that. She's one handsome female, don't you think?'

'She ain't no plain Jane, that's for sure.'

The old Briggs place was in ruins. Its adobe walls were crumbling to dust. The roof had caved in. A couple of coyotes shot out of the doorway. At the same time, quail rose into the air, their wings flapping in panic-stricken flight. If nothing else it offered some shelter from which to face the imminent foray by the Mescaleros.

Within minutes of their arriving at the abandoned station, the Indians appeared on the ridge overlooking the settlement. The men hunkered down behind any cover available, ready to let fly. All that is except Ollinger, who was secured to a fence post. He tried persuading his captors to release him to help in repulsing the common enemy. But Newcombe was having none of it.

'I'd sooner stick my head in a rattler's nest than hand you a gun,' he rasped.

'What if'n I give my word it will be returned once we've driven them off?' wheedled the outlaw.

'You heard the man,' snapped Bowdrie, grabbing the critter's shirt and shaking him. 'Now quit your griping and shut the heck up. That whining drawl is getting on my darned nerves.'

'Can you use a rifle, Mrs Lang?' Chance asked somewhat cynically.

'I'm not some helpless innocent,' she remonstrated vigorously, her hands gripping the .38 Spencer with firm determination. 'Living out here in the wilds soon toughens folks up, even a poor weak gal like me, *Mr* Newcombe.'

Bowdrie couldn't resist a mordant chuckle. 'That's put you in your place, Chance.'

'Just asking, is all,' came back the abashed reply.

The woman sniffed imperiously before moving away to take up a position behind a lump of broken wall.

There was no further time for discussion as the Indians made their first sortie. They circled around the crumbling adobe structure loosing off an amalgam of arrows, lances and bullets. The latter were old single-shot Springfields. The defenders were well ensconced and easily beat off that initial assault on their position.

But Hachita was not for giving in that easily. He kept his men well back. It was a tactic intended to waste the ammunition of the defenders. The next attack adopted a similar procedure. Many bullets were fired without any success. Not a single Indian was struck down.

It was only after the third rush that Newcombe cottoned to Hachita's wily ploy.

'That chief ain't no tenderfoot at this caper,' he called out to his old buddy. 'He's playing a waiting game, hoping that we run out of ammo. He's gotten us pinned down here too. And he knows it. We can't move, but he can send scouts off to rally more support.' The hunter's gaunt features were testimony to his apprehension that they were in one heck of a tight spot.

'You have any ideas?' muttered Bowdrie. 'I only have a handful of shells left.'

'Same here,' concurred Whipcord. 'We could make a break for it.'

The suggestion was met with louring scepticism. 'They'd chop us down afore we'd gone fifty yards,' Newcombe grunted. He peered out towards where Hachita was rallying his troops. 'Looks like that chief is building up to the final countdown.'

The low chant of ululating voices drifted across the barren landscape. Haunting and mesmeric, the chilling refrain was meant to unnerve their opponents. It was accompanied by the steady throbbing of a war drum. Whipcord shivered. It was certainly having the desired effect on him.

'He's sure gotten more brains than I credited him with,' Newcombe conceded. 'This could be their main charge. Hachita knows that this time he will suffer casualties. That's why he's girding them up in preparation for the attack.'

Hard faces, set like stone, turned to face the imminent affray. The three men were well aware that this could be their final moments on this earth. Bowdrie turned to his old pal. He held out his hand. 'No hard feelings?'

Newcombe's mouth curled in a half smile. They shook. 'No hard feelings.'

Knowing that any hope of rescue by his brother was now little more than a daydream, Caleb Ollinger threw his opinion into the melting pot. 'All that Indian chief really wants is the woman. If'n we send her out there, he'll more than likely call it a day and leave us alone. That's the only way we'll get out of here alive.'

Newcombe was on his feet in a moment. A solid back-hander sent the cringing rat flying. 'That's the cheap lowdown kind of answer I'd expect from a yellow belly like you. I ought to fill you with lead right now.' His gun was out, cocked and ready to deliver the fatal round. 'Dead or alive. That's what it says on the poster.'

It was Bowdrie who stayed his hand. 'Don't waste your bullets on him, Chance. We're gonna need every single one. And anyway, he ain't worth the steam off'n your shit.' He tipped his hat to the lady. 'Pardon my language, ma'am. But skunks like this don't come any lower in the pecking order.'

The woman acknowledged both men's gallant gesture. Now it was her turn to join in the macabre conversation regarding their tentative situation. 'Maybe I could have the answer to our predicament,' she announced, somewhat diffidently.

NINE

SQUEALERS

A set of quizzical looks silently urged her to expand on the unexpected declaration. 'Tom, my husband, once told me how he managed to drive off a bunch of Arapaho bucks that had him trapped while out scouting for the army. It scared the living daylights out of them. That was up in Wyoming before I met him. I'd forgotten all about it, never having had the need until now.'

'Get on with it, woman,' urged the bounty hunter with an impatient grunt. 'We ain't got time for no history lesson.'

Cara threw him a mordant scowl, but nonetheless elucidated. 'If'n you bore a small hole in the end of a bullet, it makes what they call a *squealer*. I've never seen them in operation. But Tom swore that it worked.' She delved into a bag containing her bits and pieces. 'If'n my memory is right, I kept them in this bag.' The others waited on tenterhooks, somewhat sceptical of the claim, yet nonetheless intrigued. Anything that offered a solution had to be worthy of consideration. 'Here they are,' she said, withdrawing four bullets. Each had been drilled precisely. 'But they only fit the Spencer.'

'How exactly do they work, ma'am?' asked a puzzled Whipcord Shorthand, fingering one of the .38 calibre bullets like it was a precious gem.

'Reckon I know,' said Newcombe. 'It's the wind blowing through the bullet at high speed, acting like a whistle. That right?'

'According to Tom its more like a high-pitched scream that goes on until the bullet's velocity is expended.'

'Here they come!' Bowdrie shouted out. 'Looks like we're gonna find out if'n they can do the business sooner than we figured.'

'Buzz one of those bullets over their heads,' Newcombe shouted. 'Then we'll find out if'n their magic works on these jaspers. Mescaleros are a suspicious set of dudes. Scaring them ain't gonna be so easy.'

Without further ado, Cara Lang slotted a bullet into the breech and let fly in the general direction of the rampaging band of Indians. Just like she said, it screamed like a banshee as the wind caught the hole bored in its nose.

'And another one, ma'am,' hollered Newcombe. Even though he was loath to admit it, he was impressed by the startling demonstration.

Again, the howling screech zipped over the heads

of the startled redskins. From an organized band of fearsome Apaches intent on death and destruction, they had suddenly degenerated into a rabble of superstitious natives.

'Aaaaaagh!' yelled one leading warrior, reduced to panic. 'The air screams at us. What is happening?'

Hachita was just as frightened by this sudden shift in fortune as his men. 'Retreat brothers, retreat!' he ordered. 'The white eyes have called up their evil spirits to destroy us. We cannot fight demons. Flee before we are overcome.'

A third bullet was enough to completely unsettle these normally solid combatants, now reduced to little more than frightened children.

The defenders were on their feet dancing about in glee as the terrified Indians scuttled off in panic-stricken disarray.

'Yahoo!' howled Shorthand. 'Gotta hand it to you, Mrs Lang, that certainly was the best magic trick I ever did see. Them squealers sure are some'n else.'

'Do you think they will return?' she asked. 'I only have one bullet left.'

'Indians are very much influenced by what they think of as the mystical world,' Newcombe remarked. 'I don't reckon they'll be back now. That sure was some stunt. I thought I'd heard everything. But your husband must have been one special guy, ma'am. I take my hat off to his memory.'

Cara slumped down on the ground gasping for

breath. The hideous slaying of Tom, followed by this near-death experience was more than heart and soul could bear. All the tension of recent days poured forth as the flood gates opened. It was Stag Bowdrie who offered sympathy and a benevolent shoulder to cry on. He held the woman close and was clearly loving every moment.

All too soon it came to an abrupt end as Cara realized what was happening. She quickly shrugged him off and stood up, moving apart to compose her thoughts.

Unaware of the sudden tension from this new quarter, Chance Newcombe studied the terrain for signs of movement.

Cara quickly pulled herself together. Preparing the evening meal helped keep her mind occupied. It was a simple affair made all the more palatable following their unexpected reprieve, care of the ubiquitous squealers. Even Caleb Ollinger was in upbeat mood. Especially seeing as he had been released temporarily to relieve himself and walk around.

The young outlaw sensed that his moment of destiny was close at hand. It was some time later when the men were sitting round the campfire smoking that Ollinger made his move.

Cara was clearing away the dishes. Nobody was paying any attention to the young killer. They were too busy congratulating themselves at having thwarted the Apaches with those wacky bullets. The outlaw certainly wasn't complaining either. Those crazy squealers had sure saved their bacon. Now they were going to be the means of his ticket out of here.

Ollinger threw a look of contempt at the preening dupes. The stupid clowns had no idea what was about to hit them.

All the while he had been gingerly shifting his position over to where a lone rifle was resting against the broken outer wall of the station. In the euphoria of their unwitting escape from a violent end, the gun had been overlooked. Foxy eyes were studying every movement of his captors. It was when Newcombe went across to check on the horses that the young killer saw his opportunity.

Effecting a casual ease, he levered himself up and strolled across. A quick grab of the rifle and he jammed the barrel into Newcombe's back.

'One false move, bounty man,' he hissed out, 'and your days are numbered. Now keep them mitts high.' Newcombe's whole body tensed, but he had no option but to comply with the young tough's guttural command.

Then Ollinger jabbed the barrel of the Winchester into Newcombe's back. 'Now all you turkeys move over to that corner where I can see you.' The jabbing rifle emphasized the gravity of his deadly threat. 'And don't be tempted to play the hero or bounty boy gets a sore head.' For a moment nobody moved. The shock of this sudden switch in providence had stunned them.

'You hear what I'm saying, knuckleheads?' The menacing rasp backed up by a Winchester carbine poking at

Chance Newcombe saw Bowdrie and his partner raising their hands. 'You too, Mrs Lang. Reckon you've given these turkeys a lesson in Indian fighting they won't never forget. But I can't have you taking the law into your own hands, can I?'

'You ain't going nowhere, Caleb.' It was Stag Bowdrie who took a pace forward. 'That gun is empty. Nobody bothered to reload it after the fight.'

'You're bluffing,' Ollinger sneered, tucking himself in behind Newcombe's broad back. 'Well it won't work. I ain't got nothing to lose. So shuck those hoglegs rapido or Newcombe here is the first to die.'

'Did you honestly think we would leave a loaded rifle within easy reach of a turnip like you?' mocked Bowdrie. He knew that a deadly game of cat and mouse was being played out here. 'We ain't greenhorns. That was the first thing I checked after those Mescaleros quit the scene. I figured out exactly what path your scheming mind was heading down. And I was proved right.'

'I never saw you go anywhere near this gun.' But Ollinger was now less sure of himself. A bead of sweat glistened on the end of his nose. It dripped off onto his hand. A factor noted by Bowdrie.

'You got eyes in the back of your head?' He offered a nonchalant shrug of disdain. 'Looks like there's only one way to find out.' He took advantage of the killer's uncertainty to draw his own gun. 'We have a showdown here. They call it a Mexican stand-off.' He paused to allow the significance of their situation to sink in. 'You pull that trigger, you're a dead man. Don't matter none if'n Chance here kicks the bucket or not, there's a hunk of lead with your name on it. You prepared to take the risk?'

Ollinger puffed out his chest, trying to deliver a tough message by jabbing Newcombe with the barrel. 'I could just as easily drill you once this guy eats dust.'

Bowdrie's diamond-hard gaze never flickered. He racked the hammer of his revolver back to full cock. 'Don't forget that Whip here is also on my side. So what's it to be, punk? I'm going to count to three. And if'n you ain't lowered the rifle by then … One.'

Tension you could cut with a knife enveloped the bleak location. Everybody was holding their breath, waiting. Nary a muscle moved. It was a scary moment.

'Two.'

The howling of a distant coyote went unheeded. Sweat had broken out on Newcombe's forehead. His craggy face gave nothing away, but the tightness of the jawline was clearly evident. Nervous glances passed between the other watchers. Who would give way first?

'Thr—'

It was the kid who backed off. Slowly, as if reluctant to display any fear, he lowered the rifle. A collective sigh of relief issued from dry throats, not least from Chance Newcombe.

'Hand it over to me,' rapped Bowdrie, stepping forward. Once he had taken possession of the long gun, he held it up and pulled the trigger. The loud blast startled them all. Only Stag Bowdrie appeared unfazed by the stark incident. 'Well I'll be a horned viper,' he jokingly breezed. 'Guess I was mistaken after all.' A mirthless chuckle followed. 'At least you're still breathing, Caleb. Don't know for how long though.'

The burning look thrust at his partner was much less conciliatory. Shorthand's face took on the colour of a setting sun as Bowdrie tossed the rifle his way. 'I think this is your'n, partner,' he added.

The lanky Shorthand knew it was his carelessness that had precipitated the near-fatal exchange. 'S-sorry about that, Stag,' he mumbled. 'I must have been carried away by the effect of them squealers.'

'Reckon you won't be so accommodating to Mr Ollinger here the next time he figures to get the drop on us ... will you, Whip?' The softly delivered rebuke was all the more potent for its lack of acrimony.

Newcombe nodded his agreement.

But he was much less forgiving to the jasper who had suckered him. He spun on his heel and delivered a full-bodied right hook to the killer's jaw. Caught off guard, Ollinger lurched backwards, falling over an old log where he lay on the ground moaning. 'Don't ever pull a stunt like that again,' the hunter growled out, hovering over the cowering brigand like a predatory eagle. Tight fists were clenched in fury ready to deliver more of the same. 'Next time you try bugging me I will ensure you never reach Carrizozo, nor anywhere else save the nearest hanging tree.'

Ollinger scrambled away from the louring threat to his continued well-being. Newcombe stepped forward intent on continuing the pasting. But just as quickly as it had flared up, like a desert sand storm, the all-consuming rage blew itself out. Newcombe hawked a lump of phlegm onto the ground at the brigand's feet.

'Ah, to hell with it. You ain't worth the bother,' he sneered.

His scornful chastisement, however, was not over yet. And it was towards Whipcord Shorthand that it was aimed. The bounty hunter was much more forthright in his condemnation of the guy's negligence. 'Carelessness like that almost gotten me killed, fella,' he snapped out, pointing an accusatory finger at the quaking Shorthand. 'Anything else like that and it'll be you that's hung out to dry. Get my drift?' He didn't wait for a reply. 'I never was one to suffer fools gladly. Ask your pal here.' Then he stumped off to go check on their horses.

The late shadows of a setting sun had enveloped the old station before Newcombe eventually regained his composure. Behaving as if nothing had happened, he declared that they would be safer staying the night at the Briggs place. Although a doubtful possibility, the Apaches might have gathered up their scattered nerves and make a return visit to finish the job. 'You can take first watch, Whipcord, and this time …' He left the sentence incomplete. The implication was clear.

'Don't you worry, Mr Newcombe sir,' he burbled out,

anxious to rebuild bridges. 'Nobody will sneak up on us while I'm on duty.'

Chance gave Whip's meek assurance the hint of a smile, satisfied that a valuable lesson had been learned.

TEN

McGURK TAKES A HAND

The rider was heading south at a steady lick. A merciless glint in the single eye probed the landscape ahead. Waco McGurk's warped features were set hard as stone. After months of fruitless searching, he had at last discovered where his nemesis was hanging out.

A bartender in the town of Cuba had told him that Stag Bowdrie was heading south for Carrizozo. And the snake had gotten himself a partner, a simpleton going under the handle of Whipcord Shorthand. McGurk couldn't resist a chortle. What sort of dippy name was that? But the moment of levity was short-lived. No matter who Bowdrie was with, McGurk would soon have the critter in his sights.

He had been trying to divest himself of the Mad Dog reputation. That kind of status had been fine and dandy during the war, and then afterwards while bulldogging the Green Hawks into submission. But those days were over. The gang had split up over a year before. Carrying the notoriety of a crazy man slung round your neck attracted too much hassle. It was aggravation that he could well do without now that he was operating alone.

The smile disappeared, replaced by a brutish scowl of hatred. All that mania for bloodletting had been revitalized. It was only by luck and a competent sawbones that he had survived the gunfight in Dodge City. His right arm would never be the same again. At nights camped out in the open, it pained him something awful. Sleep often eluded him. Those were the times when the Mad Dog's thirst for revenge was at its most virulent.

Following his recovery, McGurk had ridden back to where the rest of the gang had camped out in a shallow draw out on the prairie. They were nowhere to be seen. The gunfight and his shooting down had clearly scared the yellow rats off. Well, who needed cheapjacks like them anyway? Certainly not Waco McGurk.

That was the moment he decided to work alone, and dedicate himself to catching up with Bowdrie. He had concentrated on the new gold strikes. Taking out lone prospectors on their way to cash in their paydirt had proved surprisingly lucrative.

A jolt from his stumbling horse sent a stab of pain lancing through his shoulder. He cursed at the rat who had been the cause. 'And it won't be a fast exit for you, asshole,' he muttered under his breath. 'No sirree. And I'll relish every darned moment watching your lights go out.'

The irksome pain was a potent reminder, if'n he needed one, that kept his perverse mind in focus. The injury had meant he was no longer able to use the right hand effectively. Months had been spent perfecting a left-hand draw from a crossed holster. During that time he was forced to lie low. Now he was more proficient than he had ever been. And it was all due to the fixation for revenge that was driving him forward. He just needed to ensure nobody was lurking on his left side, which was like a blank wall due to the patch.

To prove his gunslinging skills were proficient, the Colt revolver was whipped out, cocked and aimed at a prairie dog that had just poked its head above ground. The gunman's finger tightened on the trigger. But there it remained. Shots from the far side of a low ridge stayed his hand. He drew to a halt, listening intently. And those Indian war whoops sounded like a battle was taking place.

He nudged his mount up the facing slope to the crest of the ridge. Down below in a shallow amphitheatre, a party of Apache bucks were circling a dead horse behind which three men were sheltering. If'n there was one thing Waco McGurk detested more than Stag Bowdrie, it was Indians. Tribal affiliation was irrelevant. To him they were all the same. Where Waco McGurk was concerned, the hue of their skin was like a red rag to a bull.

These were Mescalero Apache, a particularly war-like breed. His principal loathing, however, was reserved for the Pawnees who had massacred his home farm in

Nebraska and killed his parents. It was only by hiding under the carcass of a butchered pig that he had escaped alive.

The cornered jaspers down below were fighting back. But their situation was perilous in the extreme. The assailants might only have primitive arms in the form of old Springfields, but they had the numbers. One guy had already bitten the dust. There were only three left with precious little cover.

Should he intervene? McGurk was undecided. He was only one man. He could just as easily ride away. This was no business of his. Interfere and it could be his hair gracing an Apache war belt.

There again, he had three vital elements in his favour. He hated Indians with a vengeance; the element of surprise was on his side; and best of all, he had recently acquired the latest Winchester '73 that had yet to be tested in combat. The decision was made. He left his horse ground-hitched and scuttled down the slope until he was close to the action. None of the attacking force spotted him. All their attention was focused on the three cowering fugitives.

There he hunkered down behind a rock and checked that the cartridge slide was full.

Taking careful aim, he pumped three bullets in rapid succession at the mounted bucks. All three hit their target. The victims threw up their arms and tumbled off their ponies. He smiled grimly. This long gun was certainly living up to the advertising publicity. It was only when another two joined their buddies in a visit to the Great Spirit that the leader realized he was under attack from a different quarter.

Emboldened by the triumph of his incursion, McGurk moved closer. He waved an arm to the trapped men, receiving a grateful acknowledgement. The rate of fire increased as the advantage quickly swung in favour of the white men.

This sudden intervention threw the Indian attack into disarray. Hachita was now down to half his original force. A wise leader always knows when to retreat. He called his braves off and they quickly disappeared in a cloud of dust, persuaded by a further flurry of angry leaden hornets.

The three men emerged, breathing deep. They were utterly spent but noticeably relieved at having avoided a scalping.

'Boy, am I glad to see you, mister,' the grateful speaker blurted out. He was a tall figure with a thick black moustache sprinkled with silver. He had a lean hungry look, the hollow eyes and sunken cheeks giving him a melancholic brooding aura. But it was the livid scar standing proud above his right eye like an albino worm that marked him out.

'Figured we were goners for sure when those Apaches surprised us. Reckon we owe you.' He held out his bony hand. 'The name's Pake Ollinger. This is Shifty Simms,' he said indicating the older man who was reloading his gun. Simms nodded. 'And that guy is Delta Jack.'

The latter was checking on their dead comrade. 'Looks like Ten Sleep has pegged out,' the outlaw declared morosely.

Simms on the other hand was more interested in the sudden appearance of their liberator. He was avidly perusing the guy's gnarled features. 'Don't I know you from some place, mister?' His wrinkled face creased in thought. 'Seems like we've met up. I just can't recall where.'

'Don't know about that, fella,' replied McGurk with nonchalant aplomb. 'Once encountered, guys don't usually forget me.'

Simms scratched his head in thought. Then it came to him. The beard had gone, and the long hair. But that beady stare coupled with the eye patch was a dead give-away. He snapped his fingers as the memory returned.

'Mad Dog McGurk! I was in Wichita the time you shot up the piano in the Star Continental theatre. The keyboard man wouldn't play the song you requested. Claimed it wasn't on his play list for the night.' Simms couldn't resist a brisk chuckle. 'Boy, the look on that guy's face when his piano disintegrated all around him was some'n to behold.'

Pake Ollinger's eyebrows lifted in favourable sur-prise. Who hadn't heard of the infamous butcher?

McGurk's face also lit up. He was glad to be among like-minded spirits. So he enthusiastically filled them in on the exploit raised by Shifty Simms.

He finished with a breezy punch line. 'If'n there's

one thing that bugs me its entertainers that won't entertain.' Guffaws all round. But the newcomer finished his story by tempering his elation with a degree of reticence. 'It's just plain old Waco now. That label was having a bad effect on my health. So I ditched it. Be obliged if'n you guys would do the same.'

Pake Ollinger and his two surviving buddies eyed the newcomer quizzically. McGurk was eager to relieve their mystification. 'Too many guys itching to see how blamed mad I could get. It was becoming a darned nuisance, interfering with the more important business of making money. So I bought 'em all a one-way ticket to Boot Hill.'

'Sure thing … Waco. Anything to oblige the guy that saved our bacon,' concurred Ollinger as they shook hands. 'Now that poor old Ten Sleep has departed, I could use a guy with your special talents. They say you can sniff out a well-stocked bank like a bear finds honey. And you ain't too bothered about how it's knocked off. So what do you say?'

McGurk considered the offer. 'Pake Ollinger. Yeh! I've heard good things about you as well. I'd be obliged to ride along. You heading somewhere in particular?'

Ollinger scowled. 'Some bounty hunter has arrested my brother, Caleb. We've all been on vacation for a few months.' He threw a sly wink McGurk's way. 'You know what I mean. And were supposed to meet up in Roswell. Caleb got into some bother with these two dudes while they were passing through Carrizozo. They were forced to go on the run. But this bounty man tracked them down. The boys here gave him the slip. But Caleb wasn't so clever. We were figuring to catch up with them tomorrow when those Indians hit us. He goes by the name of Newcombe.'

McGurk's ears pricked up. 'Newcombe, you say. That wouldn't be Jake Newcomb, would it?'

'One and the same,' replied Ollinger, noting the newcomer's sudden interest. 'You know this guy?'

'He was bossing a gang I ran with called the Green Hawks but didn't cotton to me joining up.' McGurk huffed at the recall giving an indifferent shrug. 'It's a long story. Maybe I'll tell you about it sometime. But I sure won't be too fussed about helping you fix Mr Newcombe. Anybody that objects to my company is asking for a rattler to be stuck down his pants. These two varmints I'm tracking are headed that way as well. Bit of a coincidence us meeting up like this. Could be the gods are smiling down on good old Waco McGurk at long last.'

His mind was also running along the lines of an amnesty he had heard about for the capture of Caleb Ollinger. Maybe he could turn that to his advantage.

Ollinger sensed the legacy of the Mad Dog still actively festering inside this jigger's soul. He would need watching. But anyone who had saved his hair from being lifted was to be given the benefit of the doubt. Until he stepped out of line, Waco McGurk was welcome to ride along.

It was decided, or Pake Ollinger decided, to camp out where they were for the night. The body of the half-breed Cheyenne outlaw named Ten Sleep was covered with a pile of stones. Him and Pake had been together for upwards of three years. The outlaw boss felt that he owed him that much.

With the others standing behind him, hats in hands, the gang boss expressed his regret at the loss of the dead Indian. 'For a half-breed redskin, old Ten Sleep was a solid guy,' he intoned sombrely while standing over the rough mound. 'Knew when to keep his mouth shut. Probably 'cos most of the time he didn't cotton to what we were discussing.'

And that was it. Not much of a eulogy, but as much of a finale as guys in their profession could expect. It was always some other poor sucker who went on that permanent vacation with the Grim Reaper.

McGurk made no comment. The death of a redskin, even a half-breed, was one less for him to bother about. Had the critter survived, ructions would surely have followed. Ten Sleep was better off enjoying a permanent rest.

Over a surprisingly wholesome meal of rabbit stew, the men discussed the respective wrongs attributed to the men whom they were trailing. Shifty Simms and Delta Jack were more interested in hearing about how their new associate Mad Dog had acquired the dubious label he was now so anxious to shuck.

McGurk was initially reluctant to rejuvenate his

old lifestyle with Jersey Bob's Freelanders. But with an appreciative, almost idolizing audience to impress, how could he refuse. And he told a good story, even if it was chock full of violent and brutal anecdotes. Jack was more enthralled by these revelations than his buddy who wanted to hear about more stunts akin to the shocked piano player in Wichita. The older man enjoyed a good laugh.

Pake Ollinger was not overawed in the slightest by McGurk's colourful exposures. Even if the colour was mainly of a red hue. He was bossing this gang. And a stony regard intimated that any attempt by this dude to muscle in would meet with a swift and terminal exit.

ELEVEN

THE TRUTH DAWNS

Pake had intended to break camp early. He was eager to catch up with Jake Newcombe and set the record straight. Much as Caleb had caused him a heap of irritation on account of his twitchy pecker – this was by no means the first time he had had to ride to the young pup's rescue – he was blood kin. Their mother, God rest her soul, would have expected nothing less of him. Always look after your brother, she had told him. And he fully intended to do just that.

Although the kid could expect a severe verbal lashing once he'd been rescued with maybe some raw encouragement to curb his lustful appetite.

Unfortunately the elements chose to hinder their departure. A flash storm in the night had soaked them to the skin. With no place to shelter, the four owlhoots had been forced to hunker down beneath their slickers. The new day dawned with steam rising in clouds from the wet ground as the sun's welcome heat made its presence felt. If there was nothing else to brighten the men's mood, at least the blooming desert plants lent some appealing colour to the drab terrain.

Riding in wet duds is apt to depress a man's morale. As a result it was approaching noon before they finally rode away from the scene of the previous day's affray.

The Corona relay station was reached late in the afternoon. Seeing that it had been abandoned made the outlaws decidedly nervous.

'Looks like there's been one hellova fracas with those Indians,' observed Simms.

Although Hachita had removed his deceased brave, numerous unshod hoof prints and a couple of discarded war lances told their own tale. But most significant of all was the derelict stagecoach looking like a giant pin cushion with all those arrows skewering the woodwork. The grim sight did nought to raise the spirits of the group. Those critters were still out there some place.

'Well this ain't from no darned redskin,' declared Delta Jack reaching down and picking up an eagle feather. He handed it to Ollinger. 'Looks to me like the one Caleb had taken to wearing in his hat.'

'Maybe he dropped it deliberately as a clue so's we'd know he was here,' added Simms.

'You could be right there, Shifty,' Pake accepted. 'Unless of course he lost it in the fight. But at least we know the critters must have passed through here,' was his studied conclusion while eyeing up the discarded remnant. What he didn't know was whether the kid was still alive. An anxious look towards the three grave markers denoted his concern.

'And they've likely taken the station manager along with them as well,' mused McGurk, adding his view to the simmering pot of ideas. The guy had dismounted and was scrutinizing the roughly hewn epitaphs on the wooden grave crosses. 'And anyone else who chanced to be here when those Mescaleros hit the place. The folks in these graves are all from yonder Concord.'

Ollinger emitted an audible sigh of relief now that he knew Caleb had survived.

'The varmints we're after headed that way,' shouted the excited voice of Delta Jack, pointing to a line of shod prints making a beeline to the south-west.

'We'll stay the night here,' the gang boss announced, dismounting. 'There should be some vittles and beds available. Might as well take advantage of the Overland's generosity. And it will give us a safe haven in case those red devils come a-calling.'

There was indeed plenty of food available, not to mention a jug of home-made moonshine. That night the pursuers slept well, in proper beds and with full stomachs. An over-indulgence of moonshine meant they did not awaken until the rising sun was beaming in through an open window.

No guard had been left. It was lucky for them that Hachita had been thoroughly subdued by the white man's mystical sorcery in the form of the chimeric squealers. Not even the dawn chorus from the resident rooster had disturbed their slumbers.

Stumbling outside scratching at itchy stomachs and bleary-eyed, the four outlaws doused themselves in the station well to erase the previous night's carousing.

Like his brother, Pake Ollinger was well versed in the culinary arts so a substantial breakfast was enjoyed by all before they finally left around mid-morning. But at least their bellies were full, and morale had been fully restored. It was further enhanced by the non-appearance of the Apaches.

Pake set a burning pace to make up for lost time. The trail left by their quarry was easy to follow. Indeed, by afternoon it was becoming increasingly obvious that Newcombe and his associates had made no attempt to conceal their route. Etched boldly in the sand, even a blind man could have followed it.

The astute Shifty Simms was the first to make the poignant observation.

'That guy sure hasn't made any effort to hide his tracks,' Simms noted, scratching a pate of thinning grey hair.

'And why has he kept to the open country knowing Apaches are on the prod?' agreed Jack, equally nonplussed. 'Can't figure the sense of it. The guy don't seem to care. And he must know that we're on his trail. What do you reckon, boss?'

Pake drew to a halt. His narrowed gaze traced the line of prints deviating not a jot from the straight, and clear as daylight. A puzzled frown indicated he was equally baffled by Jake Newcombe's lackadaisical attitude.

'What's your game, mister?' he muttered under his breath.

It was Waco McGurk who provided the answer to the conundrum. 'Seems to me like Newcombe has left such an obvious trail on purpose.' The Nebraskan hard case threw Ollinger a quizzical look that sought an explanation. 'My betting is he wants us to catch him up. You got some'n to say about that, Pake?'

Ollinger drew to a halt. He pulled his hat low over narrowed eyes, focusing on the stark line of hoof prints. So that was what the jasper had in mind. Suddenly it all came flooding back to him. The incident in question had happened so long ago that he had forgotten. Too many other heinous deeds had been perpetrated since for one episode to stay lodged in the memory for long.

He nodded his understanding. 'Reckon we ain't in no hurry after all, boys. I had a run-in with the guy some years back. And I know exactly where he'll be waiting.'

The gang boss tensed noticeably, sitting astride his horse while the others waited for him to elucidate further. His face assumed a grey pallor as the grim events coalesced inside his head. But Pake Ollinger held his peace. That was one incident he would take to his grave which might not be far distant if'n that damned bounty man had any say in the matter. Well, he sure had no intention of cashing in his chips yet awhile.

It would be Newcombe for whom the bell would toll.

The years slipped away as Pake Ollinger recalled his arrival at the family home of Jacob Newcombe.

The outlaw had only recently escaped from a brutal chain gang. Luck and the Devil had been on his side. And he took full advantage to slip away, unnoticed by the sadistic guards. After only eighteen months of his sentence of ten years for armed robbery in the territorial prison at Santa Fe, he found himself unexpectedly free. It had been Newcombe who had hunted him down and been the key prosecution witness at his trial. The result was a foregone conclusion.

Free at last, Pake Ollinger would now become the hunter.

But the escape had made him a marked man. He stole a horse and quickly fled further west intending to lose himself amidst the rip-roaring frontier settlements where effective law enforcement was yet to be established. That place was in Nevada around the new gold fields of Virginia City. It was here that the fabulous Comstock Lode had been discovered.

Thousands of intrepid prospectors were flooding into the area. It offered a veritable cornucopia of easy pickings for a smart guy like Pake Ollinger. He quickly slotted back into his old ways. But the itch to avenge himself on the skunk who had put him on that brutal chain gang was ever present. It was a constant thorn in his side, an irritation that never went away. And it needed expunging.

That moment had now arrived. Ollinger had learned that Jake Newcombe was still the county sheriff based in the town of Snowflake in New Mexico territory. He had built himself a small place in a nearby valley where he ran a few head of cattle as a sideline to augment his meagre salary.

His wife Joanie took great pride in her vegetable garden. In between times she taught their 10-year-old son, Clayton, his words and numbers in a converted room dedicated to his schooling. The pair had ambitions for the boy, perhaps in the law. Though it was hoped beyond the rank of sheriff attained by Jacob. A lawyer was hinted at, perhaps eventually even a judge.

Jacob had chosen this particular woman from a mail-order catalogue of potential brides. Joanie had been a school teacher back in Kansas City. Her good looks and intelligent communication via letters meant that the pair had hit it off from the beginning. They had finally met at a halfway point in Denver.

Within six weeks of that first tryst, the pair were married. Clayton had followed almost nine months to the day later. Life could not have been more idyllic for the New Mexico lawman. They say that ignorance is bliss. It was to have devastating consequences for Jacob Newcombe.

When Ollinger arrived in Snowflake, he had hoped to finish the job quickly then disappear. But his enquiries did not yield the information he wanted to hear. The avenger was angry to discover that the sheriff was away with a posse hunting down a gang of stagecoach robbers.

Tulsa Benedict, the deputy in charge had innocently divulged that Sheriff Newcombe would be away for at least a week. He was equally verbose when Ollinger questioned him about the sheriff's circumstances.

Benedict harboured no curiosity as to why this stranger was so interested in his boss. Indeed he was glad to have the town to himself for once. It would give him the chance to make his mark. Arrest a few drunks, collect in the rents that were due. And maybe even manage to thwart a robbery. The gang that the sheriff was pursuing was not the only band operating in this part of the territory. A young hard case by the name of Billy the Kid was causing trouble down in Lincoln County. It would be a feather in Tulsa Benedict's hat if'n he could hog-tie that jasper.

Once the deputy had passed on the information he required, Ollinger wished him luck with his added responsibilities, somehow managing to contain his irritation that the blasted sheriff was away. He cursed aloud once outside. All hope of gunning down the bastard quickly had been thwarted. And hanging around Snowflake was out of the question. Ollinger had a price on his head. And that pushy starpacker might take to sifting through his file of dodgers.

So he opted for second best.

The thought of how he had carried out his revenge brought a coldly cynical sneer to the outlaw's hard face.

The white scar on his head appeared to wriggle like it had taken on a life of its own. No trace of any remorse was evident. Nor any benevolent feelings towards the lives he had snuffed out like candles in the wind. A guilty conscience certainly didn't prevent Pake Ollinger sleeping at night.

What he could never know, nor care about, was the reaction of his nemesis to those brutal acts of vengeance.

TWELVE

THE TRUTH REVEALED

'You still here, Whip?'

The sentry spun round, a sheepish grin on his face. 'Stag spelled me around two in the morning so I could get my head down for a few hours. I didn't want to wake you. Reckon an extra stint on guard was the least I could do to make amends.'

Newcombe's face remained inscrutable. But he was pleased to see that Shorthand had remained alert. The hours before first light were the most testing for any watcher.

'Glad to hear it,' he said gruffly. Then his tone softened. The guy was genuinely contrite. 'We all make mistakes. Main thing is to learn from them. That way you get to stay alive. Leaving a loaded gun for a prisoner to grab ain't the way for any of us to keep breathing.'

'I surely am sorry, sir. It won't never happen again.'

Newcombe accepted the apology with a brisk nod

119

before gesturing towards the far side of the relay station where smoke was drifting above the cottonwood canopy. 'Go get yourself some breakfast. Mrs Lang sure is one special cook. I never knew such good chow could be rustled up on the trail.'

'Much obliged Mr Newcombe, sir,' Shorthand grovelled, bowing so low his head almost touched the ground. 'That grub sure smells good and my stomach's rumbling louder than an angry mountain lion.'

The bounty hunter coughed to hide his amusement. 'No need to treat me like a visiting dignitary. Plain old Chance will do just fine.'

'Yes, sir ... erm I mean ... Chance,' Whipcord burbled, moving away. He still tipped his hat, a move that found the bounty man chuckling into his mug of coffee. Left alone, Chance Newcombe walked out into the open and scanned the trail along which they had come the previous day. Impish dust devils stirred in the breeze while a couple of curious buzzards floated by overhead. But of Pake Ollinger there was no sign. 'I know you're out there, fella. Take all the time you want, 'cos I'll be waiting.'

'You about ready to tell me what this is all about, Mr Newcombe?' The dulcet cadence from Cara Lang caught the solitary figure off guard. He visibly tensed. A swift recovery saw him retreating back inside the hard shell he had built around his damaged persona. 'I think we have a right to know if our lives are to be put in jeopardy to assuage your need for revenge.'

'I don't know what you are talking about, ma'am,' he disputed, trying to conceal any hint of unease that his plan had been sussed. 'I was just checking to see if'n those Apaches were still around.'

He made to move off. But the woman held his arm. 'You could say it's a woman's intuition. But I do know that something is eating away at you. Something that you have been carrying hidden away inside for too long.'

She paused, allowing her intimation to register, wondering if she had overstepped the mark. The warning issued by Stag Bowdrie came to mind. Yet still she persisted.

'Tell me to mind my own business, but I reckon you need to share the burden with someone. I have lost my husband, the man I loved dearly, in a brutal manner. And so I understand the heartache of such a loss.' Another more hesitant hiatus followed before she added, 'Was it your wife?'

When he made no attempt to deny the assumption, she squeezed his arm. It felt like a ghost come back to haunt him. A jolt that rippled through his whole body. That was how Joanie had always tried to make him see her point of view. Suddenly it felt like she was there beside him, gently coaxing him to unburden his heart.

The tough resilience held in check for so long was beginning to crack. He desperately wanted to relieve himself of the onerous yoke to someone. Why not this woman? Yet still he held back. The notion of sharing his most intimate grief with a stranger seemed somehow to be shallow, a betrayal of those he had lost.

'I understand how you must feel, the notion of being disloyal to her memory,' she said when he turned away from her. 'I'm sorry to have intruded. So I won't be bothering you again.'

Cara walked slowly away.

'No, wait.' The behest had been summoned from deep within Jacob's inner being. What she had said was true. He did need to relieve the weight of repression that had held him prisoner for so long. 'You're right. Joanie would want me to tell you what happened.'

Another squeeze of the arm from Cara. 'I'll get us each a mug of coffee while you decide how much you want to reveal.'

He started from the beginning, brushing over his association with Stag Bowdrie and the Green Hawks, his days as a bounty hunter. The way he had met his wife was not something to be ashamed of in those days. Arranged marriages were a common enough occurrence in frontier settlements where suitable marriage partners were in short supply.

It was when he came to the angst-ridden details of his discovery at the ranch that the narration became stilted. Every word uttered became a monumental struggle. Cara was patient and sympathetic, a caring listener.

Jacob Newcombe had never recovered from the loss of his beloved wife. He found her lying in a pool of dried blood. And there was no sign of Clayton. She must have lain there for days prior to being discovered by the distraught lawman. Jacob was unable to cope with the heinous deed. His mind shut down. All he could do was lie with her clutched to his chest.

It was only when Tulsa Benedict visited the ranch to see why the sheriff had not turned in for work that practical matters such as a funeral were instigated. But that was not the worst of it. Just as traumatic was the disappearance of his son. The day after Joanie's burial, the intense heartache was multiplied ten-fold when a passing freight haulier brought in the boy's body. The guy related how he had discovered Clayton hanging from a tree not two days' ride from the ranch.

The terrible double loss sent Jacob off the rails. He attempted to erase the appalling memory through the oblivion of drink. But that only made things worse. He was heading down a trail of personal destruction. Once a garrulous and friendly guy, Jake Newcombe had become a sullen recluse, a loner.

They say that time is the great healer. All it did for Jake was make him more determined to catch the culprit and exact his own brand of retribution. And that lay well outside the law for which he had fought so hard to uphold.

As a result he handed in his notice and reverted to his old profession.

Deputy Benedict's description of the man who had enquired about his whereabouts was a dead giveaway. And now he knew the reason for the brutal reprisal.

Pake Ollinger must have escaped from the pen, found his quarry absent from home and taken out his wrath on Jacob's family. A wire to the territorial prison confirmed his suspicions. Joanie had been shot down trying to prevent a vengeful intruder kidnapping their son. Guilt weighed heavily on Jacob Newcombe's shoulders.

The years had passed by with no sign of the killer. Until now.

THIRTEEN

THE HANGING TREE

'You look like you've seen a ghost, boss,' commented Delta Jack. 'Anything to do with the guy who's holding Caleb?'

Pake was given no time to reply as Shifty Simms cut in. 'You going to tell us where we're headed?' the aging owlhooter asked. 'Reckon we have a right to know if'n there's a showdown coming.'

'You guys will find out soon enough.'

The gang boss ignored Delta Jack's enquiry. He had no intention of elaborating. That was between him and Jake Newcombe. His thoughts once again hovered on this unexpected change of circumstances. From a simple pursuit to wrest his wayward kin from the clutches of a bounty hunter, it had become a personal vendetta.

The notion sent a shiver down his spine as he thought back to that critical moment. Once the ruthless act of vengeance had been carried out, he gave no thought as to what the outcome would be. Consequences were of no concern to a man with hate burning away at his soul. All that had been on his mind at the time was the compelling urge for retaliation against the man who had put him on that heinous chain gang. And if a spur was needed, those stripes across his back and shoulders were an ever present reminder. Attaining that revenge was a mission completed.

Perhaps when this business was over, he would hunt down the guard who had administered the beating and give him a similar send-off. And all for taking an extra corn dog at chow time. Ollinger scowled at the memory.

Without uttering another word he nudged his horse forward. The others automatically followed, remaining in ignorance of their leader's shocking personal exposure. Yet they still cast quizzical glances in his direction. Being left in ignorance of Pake's mysterious undertaking did not sit well on their shoulders.

The trail led them to an old abandoned relay station. The cold ashes of a fire no more than a day old brought a nod of satisfaction to Ollinger's resolute deliberation.

'They must have stayed here last night,' he said. 'We'll do the same. Soon enough to carry on in the morning. There ain't no hurry now that I know the score.'

He dismounted and walked over to the edge of the ruin, his narrowed gaze following the hoof prints heading away on the far side. Jacob Newcombe had offered a patent invitation to follow.

Once the true nature of the situation had been revealed in all its macabre glory, Pake realized that the bounty hunter had played him like a fish. And Caleb was the bait. He cursed himself as well as that fool of a brother for stumbling headlong into the net. The guy was taunting him, luring him on into what he knew was a trap. But now that he understood the direction in which Newcombe's mind was heading, at least he would be prepared when the showdown came, as it surely would.

He remained staring out into the empty sprawl of mesquite and greasewood. The swaying stems of tall yuccas waved to him. But he ignored their greeting.

A guttural snarl issued from Ollinger's throat. It was loud enough to attract the attention of his associates. But they thought better of interrupting the churning maelstrom of hate festering inside his head. 'Well, two can play at that game, mister,' he muttered under his breath. 'Pake Ollinger will be ready for whatever you're figuring to pull. And I'll be the one that walks away.'

'You guys know what this is all about?' McGurk asked his new partners as they spooned up the unwholesome concoction of fatback and beans. Once Pake realized what this was all about, he had no stomach for fancy cooking. So it was left to Delta Jack to make the best of a bad job.

The reluctant cook shrugged. He just followed and obeyed orders. He had no desire to pry into personal matters. Just so long as the dough kept rolling in from jobs sussed out by the boss, Jack was happy. Shifty Simms was more astute. He'd heard stories from other guys in their profession who had hinted that bounty hunter Chance Newcombe was on a mission. What it was, nobody had been able to discover. And it appeared that Pake was not about to enlighten them.

'All I do know is that it ain't healthy to stick your nose where it ain't wanted.' Delta Jack's implication was clear – keep your mouth shut! 'Pake don't take kindly to guys asking personal questions. If'n he wants to tell, he will in his own good time.'

The conversation faltered as each man fell back into his own contemplation of what the future might bring. McGurk knew that he was not about to become embroiled in some private blood feud crusade. He had his own reasons for trailing along with these guys. Any shootouts would be on his terms.

'I hope that slop you're stirring up ain't gonna poison me, Jack.'

The sudden interruption saw the three men staring at their leader. Simms smiled. Pake appeared to have buried his demons. For now at least.

'You know I ain't the best cook in the world, boss,' the outlaw replied, somewhat peeved. 'But with you being a mite occupied, I figured somebody had to rustle up some grub.'

'Tastes mighty good to me, Delta,' Simms praised his buddy. He took a plate and ladled out a large helping from the skillet, handing it to Ollinger.

The boss nodded his thanks. Accepting the offering, he spooned the mixture into his mouth without comment. 'Just a pinch more salt needed, is all.'

Delta nodded to his buddy. Seemed like the boss was back to his old self. So all was well with the world as far as he was concerned.

McGurk merely wrinkled his nose. Trail grub was trail grub.

Next morning, Ollinger had them up bright and early. The new sun had only just clawed its way over the eastern horizon. There was still a chill in the air. Old coffee and some cans of beans left by the previous occupants provided a meagre breakfast.

After breaking camp they mounted up.

'Time to hit the trail, boys,' he announced briskly. 'Don't want to keep this jasper waiting, do we?' No answer was expected, nor was it offered, as they spurred off. They would learn the grim details of their sinister crusade as and when Pake Ollinger was ready.

Whipcord Shorthand was leading the group of riders with his partner alongside when they crested a rise. He drew his horse to a halt atop the rim and looked down into an open sandy clearing with a circlet of trees encompassing it on three sides. In the middle stood a lone tree with not a single leaf gracing its scarred form.

But it was the sinister appearance that caught the beanpole's attention. 'Hey, Stag, don't that tree look mighty like the Good Lord's sign?'

His partner was more pragmatic. 'Looks to me more like a hanging tree. What do you reckon, Chance?' he asked his old buddy who had joined them.

The bounty hunter had purposely placed himself at the rear along with the prisoner to keep an eye on their back trail. He made no comment as a streak of forked lightning flashed across the mountains in the background. Dark thunderclouds bubbled and heaved, an ominous sign not lost on the watchers.

'Looks like a storm's brewing up,' commented Whipcord, oblivious to his partner's unknowing inference regarding the prominent landmark down below.

Newcombe passed by without comment, continuing down the slope before coming to a halt beside the dead tree. For a long minute he just sat astride the appaloosa, staring up at the desiccated branches. The stony gaze offered no indication as to the discordant conflagration of thoughts eating away inside his head.

When he finally spoke, no sign of any disharmony was evident to the others. 'We'll make camp here,' he said in a listless voice. 'Get the horses under cover of those trees.' His next order was for Shorthand. 'You take first watch up on that ridge. Any sign of riders approaching, make sure to come a-running.'

'Sure thing, Chance,' he acknowledged. 'You can depend on me.'

Bowdrie's thick eyebrows met in a suspicious frown. 'Ain't it a mite early to be setting down? Especially with Ollinger and his gang likely following those prints you

left for them.' The accusation was clear and unequivo-
cal. 'You going to fill me in on what's happening here?'

'You'll find out soon enough,' was the blunt reply
tempered with a sincere qualification. 'But I ain't
asking you to lay your life on the line. This is between
me and Pake Ollinger. What happens after that ...' He
shrugged, leaving the sentence unfinished. Nobody,
least of all Chance Newcombe, could foresee how the
coming showdown would play out.

Bowdrie scowled but made no further attempt to
prise the truth from his old pal.

And so they settled down to wait. It was a shady
arbour effectively alleviating the energy-sapping heat.
The nearby creek prattled cheerfully down a shallow
embankment. Birds warbled and sang amidst the leafy
branches of trees swaying in the gentle breeze. A pleas-
ant spot indeed. Only the disturbing presence of the
ugly tree prevented it being an idyllic spot to while away
a few hours.

Yet this was anything but a regular stopping point.
The tension was palpable. Each of those present couldn't
help but feel the antipathy growing more perverse as
the minutes passed. Even Caleb Ollinger was becoming
decidedly nervous. Muttering and grumbling to himself,
the killer stumbled about. His manacled hands were fastened by a rope to the dead tree trunk, making him feel
like a farm dog.

'Sit down and shut up, else I'll gag and hog tie you,'
Newcombe snarled out. The imminent showdown was

making him more fractious. The threatening stance effectively curtailed the outlaw's wandering. He slid down with his back to the tree, trying to appear tough yet failing miserably.

Newcombe positioned himself apart from the others. He was clearly in no mood for idle chatter. And there he sat making a point of cleaning and oiling his weapons. Bowdrie walked across and joined Cara Lang. She sure was one hell of a dame. Any guy lucky enough to have her on his arm wouldn't need to have wandering eyes ever again. He attempted to engage her in conversation.

But she refused to be drawn. All her attention was focused on the bounty hunter. The woman's anxious look held more than just a fearful regard for her own safety. Yet Bowdrie was glad that neither was it one of an amorous nature, a longing for the aloof bounty hunter. He knew the difference between emotional desire and concern for another's wellbeing. And this particular look told Stag Bowdrie that Cara Lang was fully in the picture regarding the guy's avowed intentions.

'You going to fill me in on what's bugging that guy, ma'am?' The request caught the woman off guard. 'I ain't stupid,' he added having grabbed her attention. 'Chance has told you why he is so keen for Pake Ollinger to catch up, hasn't he?' The woman eyed him reproachfully, but held her peace. A half smile broke across the guy's craggy façade. So his supposition was right on the button. 'Reckon it's only fair and right that me and Whip be told what it is we could be fighting over. You gonna spill the beans then?'

His earnest request for enlightenment was met with a look of uncertainty. Cara was well aware she had been made the confidante of the man's private anguish. It had happened the previous night when they stopped at the Briggs place. Should she respect that privilege, or did those in the firing line deserve to know the truth? If there was to be a showdown in which all their lives were in mortal danger, Stag Bowdrie surely did not deserve to be kept in ignorance.

She looked across at the bowed form of Jacob Newcombe. He had not moved. His whole attention was fixated on that dead stump of a tree. Slim hands unthinkingly caressed the cold steel of his weapons. Cara gave a slow nod of acceptance. Bowdrie did indeed merit knowing the truth.

FOURTEEN

PAKE SHOWS HIS HAND

And so she revealed the whole sorry episode as related by Newcombe. Once the grim events had been unfolded, Bowdrie thanked the woman. He knew that revealing a confidence had been a difficult decision. Nevertheless, it was the right one.

'I thank you, ma'am,' he acceded with feeling. 'I know it didn't come easy. But it was the right thing to do. Now I know what has to be done when those skunks get here.' His own hand strayed to the pistol on his hip.

Both sets of eyes couldn't help but settle on the grisly sign of death standing alone in the middle of the clearing. The haunting image of young Clayton Newcombe swinging beneath the scarred bough sent shivers of dread down their backs. Even a tough, world-weary dude like Stag Bowdrie was visibly moved by the depiction etched on the back of his mind.

The evocatively mesmeric moment was torn asunder

by an urgent whistle from the sentinel on the ridge.

Bowdrie was on his feet in an instant. His urgent gaze quickly shifted to the stationary figure of Chance Newcombe. No longer the brooding introspective, the bounty hunter had also leapt to his feet. He grabbed a hold of Caleb and hustled him over to the lone tree. In the blink of an eye, a ready-made noose concealed inside a saddlebag was removed and slotted over the killer's head.

'On your horse!' The blunt order caught the young punk off guard. Without thinking he mounted up, roughly assisted by his captor. The rest of the lariat was thrown over the horizontal bough and drawn tight. It was as if Chance Newcombe had been preparing himself for this very moment, such was the lithe efficiency of his movements. The rope's end was tied firmly to a low branch. Newcombe stepped in front of the tree holding a Winchester. And there he stood, legs apart, upright and solid as a granite statue, waiting.

Whipcord thundered down the slope, still waving his hands. 'Pake's a-coming!' he gasped out. 'And he's gotten three other dudes with him.' Reining up in a flurry of stomping hoofs, he joined his buddy. Together with Bowdrie guiding the woman, they took cover among the clump of trees closest to the hanging tree.

Fear now gripped the young tough in its terrifying claws. Suddenly the realization of his grim plight struck home. His brother had come riding to the rescue yet here he was with a noose around his neck. One quick slap on the horse's rump and he would be done for. Choking out his life at the end of a rope didn't bear thinking on. The shocking prospect brought a sudden splutter of protest.

'What in blue blazes are you doing?' The panic-stricken yelp needed no response. It was patently clear what Newcombe was planning. 'You c-can't do th-this. It's against the l-law,' he stuttered out.

That absurd assertion brought a grim bout of chuckling from the executioner. 'A mangy turnip like you talks about the law? Me, Jacob Newcombe,' he jabbed a thumb in his chest, 'I'm the darned law around here. Judge, jury and executioner.' He tugged on the rope to back up his claim, jerking the kid's neck and eliciting a pained gasp before his hold relaxed. 'But don't you fret, kid. It ain't you I'm after. That privilege is for your brother. Providing of course he does the right thing. Pake is gonna have to make a choice if'n he wants to save your miserable hide. A life for a life. That's what the Good Book says. And who am I to dispute the word of God?'

Caleb tried appealing to Bowdrie. The animosity he knew existed between the two old comrades might yet be revitalized. 'You ain't gonna let this turkey rob you of a bounty, are you mister? Go up against him and Pake'll sure make it worth your while. I'll see to it. And that's a promise.'

Bowdrie appeared to be considering the offer. It was all a charade. He hawked out a mirthless guffaw on seeing the kid's face light up. 'I reckon any promise you make will have more holes in it than my folks' old barn roof.' He purposely remained hidden from view wanting the gang boss to think Newcombe had waited at the hanging tree alone while the others continued on their way. 'More to the point, I'm mighty eager to see how Chance here aims to handle this sticky fix he's done landed himself with. Me and Whip here have us a grandstand seat to enjoy all the action. Ain't that so, partner?'

'It sure is, Stag. Wouldn't miss this shindig for a week of free partying with Red Sally over in Tucson,' the beanpole hee-hawed with glee. But just to ensure they were ready for any action coming their way, he jacked a round up the spout of his long gun.

That was when the pursuers with Pake Ollinger in the lead crested the ridge. They stopped on the skyline. Four silhouettes etched starkly against the burning orange of the western backdrop. The gang leader paused to take in the grim scene below in the clearing. And there, standing in the open, was his sworn enemy.

Nobody else was in sight. But Pake didn't give a tinker's cuss. All he was bothered about was catching up with his arch-rival. A hand strayed to his right shoulder. Slim fingers caressed the lumpy welts of badly healed scarring. The agony of the beatings on that hellish chain gang flashed anew through his tormented brain.

Pake snarled aloud, whipping out his rifle. But he knew the range was too great for an accurate shot. A growl akin to a mountain avalanche rumbled in his throat. So he had been right. This was what the bastard had been planning all along. Capture Caleb and lure his real prey into the trap. The sight of his brother sat astride his horse below the infamous hanging tree brought a lump to his throat.

The significance of Newcombe's action was not lost to the desperate villain. That was the very same branch over which he had strung up the rat's son. Well, he was not going to do the same to Pake Ollinger's kin.

Caleb's eyes lit up. 'Best set me free, bounty man, else you won't leave this place alive,' the kid scoffed, his faltering bravado rekindled at the sight of his brother and the rest of the gang.

Newcombe ignored the taunt. His whole being was focused on the man whom he had been seeking since what seemed like time immemorial.

Pake moved down the slope at a gentle trot, only stopping at the bottom on the edge of the clearing. Slowly he walked his cayuse forward until he was just outside the effective range of the carbine he could see held at the ready by Jake Newcombe. There he paused.

'You'd be advised to release my brother, Newcombe. Just ride away and we can wipe the slate clean. I have three other guns here to back me up. You don't stand a chance otherwise.' He chortled aloud at the unwitting quip. 'Reckon you've used up all your chances, mister.' The levity dissolved in an instant. 'Now you be one smart fella and set Caleb free.'

'Only way this rat gets off that roan is with his feet kicking air unless you give yourself up to me, Pake.'

Newcombe tugged on the rope eliciting a scared yelp from the recipient. Sensing the proximity of menace permeating the thick atmosphere, the horse snickered and jerked at which moment Caleb lost his nerve.

He began to blubber like a young urchin. 'Don't let him hang me, Pake.' Tears welled in his eyes. All the swagger of recent days had evaporated as he reverted to the young kid of his youth. 'I ain't ready to die.'

Newcombe sneered at the cringing braggart. 'Cut the griping, boy, and take your punishment like a man.' Then he called out across the clearing. 'This what you want to save, Pake? Don't seem worth the sacrifice to me.'

'He's blood kin,' Ollinger shouted back. 'You of all people should understand that, Jake. And I'll do anything that's needed to save him.'

'Except face me in a showdown, that it?'

Pake Ollinger knew that the time for jawing was over. He sucked in a deep breath. Spurs dug into the flanks of his horse. The startled animal reared up on its hind legs and charged at the ominous figure standing beside the hanging tree. Knees gripping the horse he stuck the rifle into his shoulder and began levering hard. Three times in quick succession the gun blasted out as he thundered across the clearing, howling like a demented spectre of doom.

Newcombe dropped to one knee as splinters of

wood plucked from the dead trunk flew around him. Unfazed by the frenzied attack, he took careful aim. His second shot took Pake's horse in the neck. It stumbled, throwing the rider off. The fallen man was momentarily stunned but quickly recovered, scrambling for cover behind the dead animal.

That was when Simms and Delta joined the affray Seeing their leader in desperate straits jolted his two loyal associates into action. Dismounting, they ran forward to where some logs provided cover.

Bowdrie and his pal now made their presence felt in devastating fashion. Caught out in the open, Delta Jack was the first to go down. The outlaw was hit in the chest by three bullets from the gun of Whipcord Shorthand before his peppered body hit the dirt.

'Good shooting, buddy,' his pard gleefully commended. 'You ain't just an ugly face.' He then joined him in laying down a field of fire against the remaining adversaries.

When the shooting started, McGurk was fifteen feet to the right of Simms sheltering behind a tree. Once he realized that the odds were much less in the gang's favour than previously assumed, he hesitated. This was not his fight. And he had no intention of getting caught up in any crossfire. It was time for him to seek out pastures new. And quickly, before things got out of hand.

Powder smoke drifted across the killing ground. In the thick of the action, nobody noticed the stealthy retreat of the wily outlaw. He took advantage of the outer layer of trees to make his way back towards the top of the ridge.

There he paused, curious to witness how things panned out.

Shots were now being exchanged between the two groups. Yet neither seemed able to gain an advantage. The battle had barely begun when a scream rent the air. Cara Lang pointed to the swaying form of Caleb Ollinger, whose legs were kicking frantically. The roan on which he had been seated had panicked as soon as the shooting started.

Seeing his kid brother choking out his life was too much for Pake. A maniacal screech of anguish pierced the fetid air as the outlaw leapt to his feet. Undaunted by the obvious danger, he dashed across the open ground. The rifle was discarded. Brandishing a pair of .44 Colt Peacemakers, he charged towards the twitching body, firing from the hip.

And he almost made it. Zigzagging to avoid flying hunks of lead brought him to within yards of his adversary. Then the inevitable happened. He took one in the shoulder from Bowdrie, which spun him around. But it was left to Chance Newcombe to despatch the object of his revulsion with a bullet in the middle of the forehead.

The hunter had one cartridge left. Turning slowly, he drilled the rope around Caleb's neck. The kid tumbled to the ground where he lay writhing like a wounded snake, desperately sucking air into tortured lungs.

With his boss down and out of the running, Shifty Simms saw no reason to continue the fight. 'OK, I surrender,' he called out anxiously, tossing his gun into the open. 'This ain't my fight. I had no idea that Pake and you had a past, mister. It was all his idea to follow you.'

'Come out where I can see you,' came the growled reply. 'And keep your mitts raised. Any tricks and you'll be joining these turkeys in the hereafter.'

'S-sure thing,' stammered the scared outlaw. 'I don't want no trouble.'

Once the aging owlhoot posed no further threat the protagonists emerged from cover.

'What's your name?' rapped Newcombe.

'Shifty Simms,' replied the morose guy. With his buddy and the boss dead, he had completely forgotten all about Waco McGurk. 'I ain't worth nothing if'n that's what's on your mind. Not like these two jaspers. The killing of that kid weren't my doing. And I told Caleb to watch himself after he shot that gambler in Carrizozo and ran the kid down.' He was desperately trying to back-pedal. True to his nickname, he wanted to shift the blame elsewhere.

'Don't matter none. You're coming with me to stand trial. If'n it's as you say, the judge will go easy on you.' He turned to Shorthand. 'Get the critter's horse and we'll be heading off.'

'Hold up there, Whip.' Bowdrie's sharp retort

crackled with suppressed hostility. 'Me and Chance here have some unfinished business that needs sorting first.' All eyes swung towards the commanding presence of the ex-Green Hawk. 'Ain't that right, old buddy?'

FIFTEEN

UNEXPECTED CONCESSION

Cara was helping the half-strangled young Ollinger to his feet when Bowdrie stepped forward to make his play. 'Reckon this is the time we part company, Chance. Me and Whip will be taking Caleb to secure our amnesty. I ain't bothered about this other dude. With no bounty on his head he can skiddadle far as I'm concerned.' His face was set in granite-hard determination. It softened momentarily. 'And I'd be honoured to have you accompany me, Mrs Lang.' Although his eyes never left those of the bounty hunter as the offer was made.

Newcombe straightened up and turned to face his rival. An equally dogged refusal to comply was written across the weathered countenance. 'Then you'd better come and take him.'

Shorthand and the woman stood to one side. Open-mouthed, unable – or in Whipcord's case, unwilling – to intervene, they could only watch and wait for the inevitable slap of hands on leather. Only the harsh croaking of Caleb's raspy breathing disturbed the tense silence that had descended over the clearing.

Up on the ridge, McGurk was likewise stunned. There standing in the open facing the bounty hunter was none other than Stag Bowdrie. Only now had the guy made his presence felt. So it was him and his pard who had ambushed the gang. They must have been hiding in the trees.

What these two old comrades were doing in this neck of the woods, and apparently in the same outfit, was not a question that presented itself to the vengeful des-perado. His hand tightened on the Volcanic repeating rifle. He only needed the one shot to take the guy out. But the distance was too great for a guaranteed hit even with such a fine rifle. Frustration twisted the scowling face.

Then he relaxed. Perhaps it was as well. He wanted to stare that skunk in the face so he knew exactly who was sending him to hell when he pulled the trigger.

A more concentrated study of the group produced a puzzled frown. Judging by the stance of the two men, it appeared to be a less than amicable liaison. Then it struck him. McGurk knew exactly what was being staged below. A walkdown! He had been in the same position on numerous occasions and was still around to know that only one of the protagonists would leave the clear-ing alive.

The question now arose. What had catapulted these

two old buddies into a showdown? Then it struck him. Had to be the amnesty he had heard about.

It was Cara Lang who broke in on the stand-off before either man could make a move. 'Hasn't there been enough killing already?' she hollered out frantically. 'You two jugheads are supposed to be old friends. Yet here you are, squaring off with the intention of shooting each other. And all over who gets the reward for taking this guy in. I've never met anybody more stubborn.' She stamped her feet, a feeling of impotent exasperation drying up the rampant tirade.

'You finished, lady?' Newcombe asked. Cara aimed a look of pure venom at the bounty hunter. Not waiting for a reply, he addressed Bowdrie in a manner that was far less threatening than it ought to be. 'Why do women never let a guy finish what he has to say? He's all your'n, Stag. I'm finished here.'

The offer was met with a bewildered lift of a sceptical eyebrow. Bowdrie's hands still hovered above the butts of his twin hoglegs. 'What you saying, Chance?'

'What I'm saying is you can have him. I don't want the critter. He was only ever the bait to lure his brother out of the woodwork.' He moved across to his saddle and heaved it onto the back of his horse. 'And now that Pake's hit the high trail, my job here is almost over. Only one thing left to do.' He didn't elaborate on what that could be. 'If'n you folks leave now, you should be in Carrizozo by sundown.'

Then he turned to face the nervous Shifty Simms.

'Stag's right. You ain't any use to me without a bounty on your head. Get your horse and ride. But stay out of trouble else I'll be coming for you. Savvy?'

'S-sure thing, mister,' burbled the stunned Simms, unable to comprehend that he was being released. 'I always intended heading for Mexico once this business had been sorted. Got me a stake down there. I'm too old for this game anymore. Much obliged.' Warily he moved away from the potential killing zone, still not sure that his guardian angel had worked her magic.

Suddenly the build-up of tension was released. A huge sigh of relief washed over all those present. 'But just so's we understand one another, Stag.' Newcombe was once again the tough bounty man. 'Like I told that jasper, you step out of line once that amnesty has been granted, and I'll hunt you down.'

'Ain't no cause for me to buck the law once I get that release document,' Bowdrie assured his compadre. 'No more dodging posses, always looking over your shoulder. Those days are over. Got me a place in the San Agustin country west of here.' A pensive stare panned across the distant rise of hills, his whole being suffused by a wistful aura of satisfaction. 'It's only small at the moment. Just a few head of cattle. But with the help of a reliable partner, we could make it a successful spread.' His gaze shifted to the bewildered Shorthand who was struggling to keep up with the rapid change of events. 'What do you say, Whip? Fancy going in with me?'

'You never told me about that, Stag,' the surprised

guy blurted out. 'Never figured you for a cattle man.'

'A fella can change. And maybe I never said anything 'cos I had to be certain you were the right guy.' Then he turned to face Cara Lang. 'All that's missing is a good woman to make it all worthwhile. I'd be obliged to look after you, ma'am. That's if'n you've a mind to become a rancher's wife.'

Cara's serene features gave no hint as to which way her thoughts were leaning. She was taken aback by the proposal. Such a momentous decision needed time to reflect on. 'Let's just see whether that amnesty will be approved before any commitments are made on either side,' she declared.

It was neither a refusal nor an acceptance. But for the moment it would have to suffice. Cara had a pragmatic head on her shoulders. If nothing else, the last few days had made her wary of anything that involved entrusting her future to another man, especially one with a shady past. She had only recently lost her beloved husband in a violent manner. That needed getting over. And only time could make it happen.

Up on the ridge, McGurk watched as Shifty Simms scrambled onto his horse and rode away. So they'd gone soft on the little runt. It didn't matter a jot to McGurk. All his attention was focused on Stag Bowdrie. And that critter also appeared to have been given a second chance.

The hard-boiled tough smiled. That was just how he wanted it. Now it was his turn. And Stag Bowdrie would not be given another break. Waco, the Mad Dog McGurk would make certain of that. Then once he had settled with Bowdrie, perhaps he would come back and even the score with Newcombe.

What McGurk witnessed next added to the mystery surrounding this whole bizarre episode. And it clearly had something to do with the guy's fixation on getting even with Pake Ollinger.

The four riders had left the clearing on their way to Carrizozo. Only Chance Newcombe remained. And there he sat for a while some distance from the hanging tree. He needed time to think. Time to allow all the hate that had built up over the years to disperse. At long last the locked door had been opened. Lonely is the hunter. And for too long Jacob Newcombe had ridden a solitary trail in search of retribution.

Now he had achieved his own personal nirvana. And it felt good. More than good; exhilarating to the point of perfection. No, that was wrong. How could anything be perfect without his beloved Joanie and young Clayton by his side? A single teardrop traced a path through the hard coating of stubble.

For ten minutes he sat there. Although it could only be second best, he still managed to find enjoyment in the sense of release. Slowly yet steadily, his body was able to relax. The killing of Pake Ollinger had been a necessary part of the healing process. Now he also would be finally permitted to hang up his guns and settle down. Like his old pal, the mundane life of regular work beckoned invitingly.

And so the final ritual had arrived. He stood up and walked across to his horse. Tucked inside the saddlebag was a bottle of coal tar oil. Unscrewing the cap, he sprinkled the contents around the base of the odious tree. That done, he scratched a match on the scarred trunk and tossed it onto the inflammable liquid. Instantly the flames caught. Soon the dead wood of the tree was burning fiercely.

The avenger stepped back and watched as the symbol depicting all his grief was consumed by the flames. Black smoke rose into the air. A drifting pyre of anguish and hurtful memories. The torment was finally over.

With the tree blackened and reduced to a charred lump, Chance Newcombe rose to his feet and mounted up. A last look, a final prayer to assuage any remaining guilt and he rode away, never to return. No turning round for a last look. The past was now behind him. The future beckoned with open hands.

Waco McGurk had waited impatiently for the man below to complete his strange but macabre task. He had no idea what it signified, nor did he care. A satisfied smile greeted the guy's decision to head east. It was the opposite direction to that in which Bowdrie and the others had gone. Now was the opportunity to make his own move without any interference from the bounty hunter.

SIXTEEN

STALKING THE STAG

The four riders had no need to hurry. It was with a light heart that Bowdrie regaled his comely associate with details of his plans for the ranch. A genuine enthusiasm held her attention.

'I've bought in some English Herefords to improve the long horn breed, give them more meat on the bone,' he enthused, waving his arms about. 'And Whip here is a dab hand at fixing things.'

'Don't forget those chickens I reared when we had that place in the Wolf Creek country,' his partner butted in. 'Best new laid eggs I ever tasted.'

Bowdrie nodded. 'I sure can't disagree with you there, buddy.' And so it went on.

Cara listened quietly, adding her comments occasionally and the odd question to clarify points. Perhaps this guy had quit his old ways for real. There was still plenty of time to make a final decision as to whether she wanted to spend her life with a reformed outlaw. At the steady pace they were travelling, it looked like they weren't going to reach Carrizozo before the next day.

It was Whipcord who drew their attention to the floating flume of black smoke drifting above the tree canopy to their rear.

'What do you reckon that is, Stag?' he asked. 'A prairie fire, d'yuh reckon?'

Bowdrie's gaze was pensive. 'Looks like Chance has put all his demons to the torch. He's set that old tree afire. A fresh start for him …' He paused, throwing a wishful eye towards his lovely companion. '… And hopefully one for us too.'

Cara merely stared at the rising cloud, but made no comment. It was she who turned back and nudged her horse into motion. The others followed, each wrapped in his own thoughts. Even Caleb Ollinger had lost his swagger knowing that his one chance of escaping justice had faded with the killing of his brother.

Paralleling their course at a higher level on a shelf of rock, Waco McGurk was scouring the landscape for a place to make his move. Things were working out just dandy. Not only was Stag Bowdrie now within his grasp, but with Pake dead, he would be able to claim the bounty on his brother in addition to applying for the amnesty. The governor had splashed notices all over the territory offering a free pardon to any gunfighter who brought in the killer of his son.

It was a unique opportunity never previously offered.

And unlikely to happen again anytime soon. Others would be after that lucrative prize. Yet he was the lucky one to have accidently tracked Caleb down. And nobody was going to stop him claiming the double reward for his trouble.

The line of four riders was crossing a level tract of white salt flats. Shorthand was in the lead with young Ollinger close behind. This was the moment McGurk had been waiting for. He spurred his horse ahead to where the shelf dipped, allowing easy access to the flats. And there he dismounted behind a cluster of boulders. Removing the Volcanic from its scabbard, he checked that the twenty-round magazine was fully loaded.

Then he selected a suitable position to halt the group in their tracks. His sights were centred on removing the guy in the lead. Shorthand's red one-piece made a perfect target onto which he now settled his sights. The shot when it came echoed across the open flats, bouncing back off the orange sandstone cliffs on the far side.

Whipcord Shorthand never knew what hit him. His corpse tumbled off the horse. Even before his dead body hit the ground, McGurk had taken out Caleb's horse. He wanted the kid alive, but did not want the kid making a run for it. The roan stumbled forward, tipping the rider over its neck and trapping him beneath.

McGurk chuckled inanely to himself. It couldn't have worked out better if'n he planted the kid there with his own hands. Two guys out of action. All he needed now was to get his hands on Bowdrie. The woman would provide some fun on the rest of the journey to Carrizozo. Then once he'd sated his lust, she would have an unfortunate accident. Only he and Caleb were going to finish the journey.

That was the plan. Now there was only Stag Bowdrie standing in the way. And the critter hadn't wasted any time reacting to the sudden violence of the ambush. Veering away, Bowdrie had dived off his horse to shelter behind a clump of organ pipe cacti. The sturdy trunks afforded excellent cover.

In the heat of the moment, the piercing sound of gunfire had panicked Cara's own horse, which made a beeline for where McGurk was hidden on the opposite side of the flats. He leapt out waving his hat in the air to confuse the animal. Although exposed to retaliation by Bowdrie, McGurk was confident that he would hold his fire for fear of hitting the woman. He grabbed a hold of the bridle and quickly dragged Cara off the horse and behind the cluster of rocks where his own securely tethered mount was snickering fearfully.

'Who are you?' Cara blurted out, her mind in a turmoil following the brutal attack. The frightening appearance of the hard case with his black patch and twisted visage blurred her thinking. The fact that he was with the Ollinger gang did not register. 'What do you want from us?'

'The name's McGurk. Some folks call me the Mad Dog.' The inane chuckle sent rampant barbs of terror rippling through Cara's sparse frame. 'So it's best not to get me riled up. Savvy? But it ain't you I'm after, pretty lady,' he sneered, keeping an eye on the organ pipes where his adversary was hiding. 'But you're going to be my ticket out of here once I've winkled that skunk out of his bolt hole.'

To ensure Cara did not pull any stunts to escape, he quickly tied her up with his lariat. Then he turned his attention to getting a bead on the real objective of his anger. Numerous shots were exchanged over the next half hour. Bowdrie was pinned down and well covered. But without water or access to anything else other than the ammunition he was carrying, the odds were clearly in McGurk's favour.

But the Mad Dog was impatient to get this over with. The longer the stalemate continued, the more chance there was of somebody stumbling on the combat zone and taking an unwelcome hand in the proceedings.

So he decided it was now time to play his ace in the pack. 'You know who it is that's gunning for you, Bowdrie? Recognize that voice, do you?'

For a moment, there was silence as the bushwhacker allowed his victim to figure it out. Then he hawked out a blood-curdling howl of delight when Bowdrie pumped a couple of shots his way. 'That's right, mister. The Mad Dog has gotten you pinned down. I've been trailing you a long time. Now you're gonna pay big time for gunning me down in that Prescott saloon.'

'And you figure on doing that with me over here and you up there?' scoffed Bowdrie. 'All I have to do is wait until dark. Then it'll be you who needs to be affeared. 'Cos I'll be coming for you. Whipcord was worth ten of your kind.'

'Maybe you haven't worked it out yet, fella,' McGurk pressed home. 'But I have the woman up here, trussed up like a Thanksgiving turkey. You don't come out into the open, she's gonna be one dead lady. And that would be a shame seeing as how I was looking forward to some fancy action once you'd joined red shirt over yonder.' He nudged Cara's foot. 'Tell him I ain't funning, lady.'

'Don't listen to him, Stag,' she hollered out forcing herself to remain calm and unruffled. 'He's bluffing. You can hold out until nightfall. And the answer is "Yes". I will go with you ...' The angry retort was cut short by a cry of pain as McGurk cuffed her around the head.

'You harm one hair of her head and I'll ...'

'You'll what, Staggy boy?' McGurk chortled inanely. 'I'm holding all the aces here. You put one foot wrong and madam gets it. So what's it to be? A life for a life, the Good Book says. Make your choice, and be quick about it. I'm getting impatient to be off claiming my dues. And that amnesty will be a welcome bonus.'

Bowdrie struggled to ignore the taunting. But his whole being was tangled up inside. With Whipcord so brutally taken out and Cara in the hands of a madman, his life felt like it had lost all meaning.

'It's mighty heart-warming to know you have feelings for me, Cara. But I don't figure he aims to let us both

156

walk away.' The words were torn from his very soul, such was his torment.

'You're darned tooting I don't, mister.' The macabre growl was delivered with menacing ease. Evil seeped from every last nuance. 'You don't come out within five minutes, the next bullet has her name on it.'

'Do I have your word, she'll go free?' Bowdrie could barely enunciate the question. An agonizing torment soured his handsome visage. He had been so near achieving his goal. Only to be thwarted at the last hurdle. His head drooped.

'All I want is you, and then to claim that amnesty with Caleb,' McGurk urged. 'The woman don't mean nothing to me.'

Bowdrie heard, but still hesitated. How much credence could be given to the pledge of a crazy madman like Waco McGurk?

Yet he had been given no choice. Stag Bowdrie was a lawless brigand with numerous bad deeds behind him. He had always expected to die with his boots on. Conversely, Cara Lang was an innocent female unwillingly caught up in this mayhem. One minute heading for a new beginning with the woman of his dreams, next facing his own exit. How could life be so cruel?

There was only one way to set the record straight.

'All right, you win. It's a deal. I'm coming out,' he croaked.

There was no point in holding on any longer. The die had been cast. Bowdrie stood up and threw his gun into the open. Then he stepped from behind the thick green organ pipe trunks.

With Cara's hands still tied behind her back, McGurk pushed her in front of him. He still did not trust the man facing him.

'That's far enough,' McGurk ordered when the two factions were no more than twenty feet apart. 'Now say your prayers.' He raised the pistol.

That was when a screaming whine whistled by overhead.

'What in hell's name …' McGurk automatically ducked down. Never having witnessed the manic screech of a squealer, he was completely disorientated.

Cara instantly recognized it to be that last bullet which she had given to Chance Newcombe along with the Springfield before they separated. She pushed McGurk away and dropped to the floor as the bounty hunter stepped out from behind the boulders recently occupied by the scheming outlaw.

'Drop the gun, mister!' Newcombe's terse directive was backed up by his trusty Remington. 'You're under arrest. And I'm pretty sure there'll be a substantial reward for bringing in a bad boy like you.'

'H-how did you know I was t-trailing these jaspers?' the killer asked, nonplussed. 'You were headed in the opposite direction.'

Newcombe's face split in a cold mirthless grin. He licked his finger and stuck it in the air. 'You should have checked the wind direction, sucker. I heard the gunfire from five miles away and came a-running. Looks like I was just in time.' The smile disappeared. 'Now drop the gun.'

As always, the chance to surrender had been offered.

'Too late for that,' McGurk balked. 'I ain't going back to the pen, or the hangman.' His gun swung, the hammer snapping back. Dead or alive was the dictate. And Mad Dog McGurk had opted for a terminal departure.

Cara shut her eyes. Her head fell onto her chest. Yet another killing. Would it never end? Bowdrie ran across and took her in his arms. For the second time in as many days, the flood gates opened. Her slim frame shuddered, torn between sorrow and relief. He stroked her flaxen hair, whispering endearments that communicated how much he cared. And this time she was more than willing to cling on to him.

It was some time before a measure of normality, if such there could ever be, was restored. In the meantime, Chance had freed Caleb and had him doing what the kid clearly did best – digging a grave for the deceased Whipcord Shorthand.

Some time later, the three associates were standing over the makeshift grave. Bowdrie said a few words in memory of his partner. Then McGurk's body was strapped to the saddle of his horse.

The two men shook hands. Once again the parting of the ways had arrived.

'You sure you don't want to ride along,' Bowdrie

pressed. 'The bounty on these two jaspers could be a sizeable reward. You deserve half of it.'

'Put my share into making that spread of your'n a going concern. I need time on my own to get things sorted out up here.' He tapped his head. Bowdrie nodded. Now that he had Cara Lang by his side, he understood perfectly. Losing the ones you love in such distressing circumstances could never be put aside. Chance Newcombe was a man alone. And like as not he always would be.

But for Stag Bowdrie, a new start beckoned. From the depths of despair to a bright future, all in the blink of an eye. Yet such is the tenuous link between life and death.

With a wave of his hand Chance turned away, heading back towards the plume of smoke still drifting above the treeline.